He Had To Have Her.

"You're used to calling all the shots, aren't you?" Rand drawled lazily. "Those poor fools you bless with your phone number and approved lunch dates really don't stand a chance with you at all."

"And those poor dimwits who fall for your smooth operator act don't stand a chance with you, either," Jamie retorted.

Common sense told her to stop this at once. The tension between them was tangible and pulsing with excitement. But she couldn't seem to stop herself.

His lips curved into a sexy smile. "Maybe you're immune to *others of my ilk*, but you're far from immune to me, honey. We proved that yesterday." He cupped her shoulders with his hands and slowly drew her toward him. "I think you want me to prove it again."

"I do not!" But tendrils of heat were uncurling in her abdomen, growing hotter and tighter.

He lowered his head to hers....

Dear Reader:

Sensual, compelling, emotional . . . these words all describe Silhouette Desire. If this is your first Desire, let me extend an invitation for you to sit back, kick off your shoes and enjoy. If you are a regular reader, you already know what awaits you—a wonderful love story!

A Silhouette Desire can encompass many varying moods and tones. The books can be deeply moving and dramatic, or charming and lighthearted. But no matter what, each and every one is a terrific romance written by and for today's women.

I know you'll love March's *Man of the Month*, *Rule Breaker* by Barbara Boswell. I'm very pleased and excited that Barbara is making her Silhouette Books debut with this sexy, tantalizing romance.

Naturally, I think *all* the March books are outstanding. So give into Desire . . . you'll be glad that you did!

All the best,

Lucia Macro
Senior Editor

BARBARA BOSWELL
RULE BREAKER

SILHOUETTE *Desire*

Published by Silhouette Books New York

America's Publisher of Contemporary Romance

SILHOUETTE BOOKS
300 East 42nd St., New York, N.Y. 10017

ISBN: 0-373-05558-7

First Silhouette Books printing March 1990

Printed in the U.S.A.

BARBARA BOSWELL

loves writing about families. "I guess family has been a big influence on my writing," she says. "I particularly enjoy writing about how my characters' family relationships affect them."

When Barbara isn't writing and reading, she's spending time with her *own* family—her husband, three daughters and three cats, who she concedes are the true bosses of their home! She has lived in Europe but now makes her home in Pennsylvania. She collects miniatures, holiday ornaments, tries to avoid exercise and has somehow found the time to write over twenty category romances.

One

"She said no."

Rand Marshall heard the note of shocked disbelief in his friend's voice and suppressed a smile. Handsome, successful and infinitely eligible, Daniel Wilcox was unaccustomed to hearing the word no from anyone—particularly not from a she.

"Who said no?" asked Rand. They were snacking on Buffalo chicken wings at a popular restaurant while waiting for their dinners to arrive. At seven o'clock on a Thursday night, the place was nearly deserted and conversation was possible, unlike weekend nights when the place was packed to overflowing with the professional young singles crowd and live music.

"*She* did. You know, Jamie Saraceni. The one I've been talking about for the last three weeks." Frowning, Daniel reached for another chicken wing.

"Ah, yes, the incomparable Jamie." This time Rand didn't bother to hide his smile of sympathetic amusement.

"For the last three weeks, I've been listening to you map out your campaign to lure the elusive Jamie into your bed. And after all your efforts, she said no?"

"Into bed? Ha! I've spent the last three weeks trying just to get her to go out with me," Daniel corrected glumly.

Rand glanced at him with genuine surprise. "You mean you haven't been able to get a date with her?"

"Not one." Daniel snatched another chicken wing, his sixth from the plate of eight. Clearly, he was eating to cope with his stunning setback. "I sent her roses, candy, balloons. Funny cards. Cute stuffed animals. I've called her every day, sometimes twice. I even managed to get two tickets to a Broadway show in New York. Told her we could drive up for the show, have a late dinner and stay overnight at the Plaza Hotel. What woman do you know who could resist that?"

"But she said no?" Rand watched Daniel gulp down another chicken wing. "No to everything?" He was more than a little amazed himself.

"No to everything," Daniel affirmed gloomily. "Rand, do you think she actually meant it when she said that she wasn't interested in dating me?"

Only a thirty-four-year-old bachelor with approximately twenty years of successful dating behind him could seriously ask that question after such solid evidence of rejection, Rand thought. That was Daniel. But in all honesty, it was himself as well.

He frowned thoughtfully and looked at Daniel, whom he'd known since their college days. Daniel was still the boyishly good-looking, well-dressed, well-built guy he'd always been. He was a highly successful dentist, relying on his charm as much as his skill to build a large practice. There had never been a woman he'd wanted whom he hadn't had.

Until now.

"Maybe she's playing hard to get," Rand suggested.

"I thought that, too, at first," Daniel intoned miserably, reaching for another wing. Finding they were all gone, his gloom visibly deepened. "But when she turned me down for the Plaza Hotel...that's when I started to think that maybe she really doesn't want to go out with me." He heaved a heavy sigh. "I'm not used to rejection, Rand. I didn't recognize it for what it was."

"Maybe she's involved with someone else," Rand interjected tactfully. He was also having a bit of a problem interpreting this situation, for Rand Marshall was equally unfamiliar with feminine rejection.

Daniel shook his head. "No, she's not, I know that for a fact. My dental hygienist, Angela Kelso, happens to be a friend of hers. In fact, that's how we met. Jamie brought her nephew to me for a consultation, referred by Angela."

"And it was lust at first sight," Rand concluded. "On your part, at least."

"Angela told me that Jamie isn't even *dating* anyone right now. I thought all I'd have to do is ask and..." Daniel dramatically clutched his head with his hands. "Maybe I'm finally starting to lose it, Rand. Maybe I've finally reached the stage my parents have been warning me about all these years...you know, the if-you-keep-playing-the-field-eventually-all-the-good-ones-will-be-taken-and-you'll-wind-up-alone stage." He shuddered. "Is this nature's way of telling me if I don't get married and settle down now, I'll end up some pathetic old bachelor that half the world pities and the other half assumes is gay?"

"You are starting to lose it if you buy that old saw." Rand grinned. "Forget this Saraceni babe. Call someone else right now. I guarantee you'll have a date within ten minutes. And forget all about that pathetic old bachelor nonsense. I did, years ago."

"Your family gave you the same spiel, huh?"

"Worse. I didn't buy it then and I don't buy it now. It's pure scare tactics to force us to fit into the mold they've designed for us."

And Daniel didn't know the half of it, thought Rand, smiling cynically. Daniel's family was pleased with his choice of dentistry as a vocation, pleased with him as a person, as a son. It was only his freewheeling bachelor life-style that the elder Wilcoxes disapproved of.

However, *his* parents, Dixon and Letitia Marshall, disapproved of everything about their son Rand. Cranking out lusty potboilers was not their idea of a tasteful, respectable way to earn a living, however profitable it might be. And it was profitable. Rand's latest effort had netted him an advance in the high six-figure range, which royalties would push over the million mark.

Still, the Marshalls of Ablemarle County, Virginia, were not impressed. They already had money, old money, and their blue-blooded lineage could be traced directly to the first families of Virginia. Rand's sexy thrillers and liberal life-style were far too... red-blooded for their tastes. Years ago they'd begun to consider Rand, their second son, who'd been an afterthought, as an unfortunate mistake as well. Their firstborn son, Dixon Junior, was, as he'd always been, the fulfillment of their parental dreams.

Rand directed his wandering mind back to Daniel and the problem at hand. Always pragmatic, he preferred dealing with situations that could be resolved. His differences with his family didn't fall into that category. "Do yourself a favor and make a date for tonight," he told Daniel. "You need to have your confidence restored. Call a woman you know will be thrilled to hear from you."

"Maybe you're right." Daniel sounded doubtful but less morose.

"Of course I am." Rand gave his friend a fraternal pat on the shoulder.

"I could call Mary Jane Strayer. She's broken other dates to go out with me."

"Great! Call her now. Set something up for later tonight. There's a pay phone in the back of the restaurant."

"I guess I will. Jamie Saraceni missed her chance. There'll be no more calls from me to the Merlton Library."

"The Merlton Library?" Rand echoed, confused.

"It's where Jamie works. She's the children's librarian there. It was the only place I could call her. Her home phone is unlisted, and she wouldn't give me the number," he added, a bit sheepishly.

"The babe's a *librarian*?" Rand chuckled.

"Sure, have a good laugh," grumbled Daniel. "I bet you couldn't get a date with Jamie, either. After all, you're as smooth, superficial, arrogant, aggressive and self-satisfied as I am."

"Are all those adjectives hers?"

Daniel nodded his head vigorously. "She used them every time I asked her why she wouldn't go out with me. She claims that our type revolts her."

"You know, I'm beginning to get the feeling that this definitely isn't a game of hard to get. The lady librarian really means it. My curiosity is thoroughly aroused." Rand's smile resembled that of a crocodile who'd just spotted his next meal. "It might be worth a trip to the Merlton Library to see this bibliophilic goddess."

"Go ahead," Daniel said with undisguised eagerness. "I'd love to see you get shot down in flames, too."

"Daniel, old buddy, the woman who'll shoot me down has yet to be born." Rand grinned. A gleam shone in his light brown eyes. "And if that sounds smooth, superficial, arrogant, aggressive and self-satisfied, so be it."

"We'll see how arrogant, self-satisfied, et cetera, et cetera, you feel after Jamie Saraceni has put your ego through the shredder." The prospect seemed to please him, and Daniel smiled for the first time that evening. "I think I'll call Mary Jane now."

Daniel left the table, a renewed swagger in his stride. Rand grinned. The librarian had dealt a severe blow to his friend's male pride, but Wilcox was recovering fast.

Then Rand's eyes narrowed thoughtfully. Daniel Wilcox, one of the most sought-after bachelors in the Philadelphia-South Jersey area, had flipped over a woman who wouldn't even give him her phone number. She'd successfully rebuffed a courtship campaign that had proven fool-proof with other women over the years. Rand pondered the amazing facts. Who was this woman?

Daniel returned from making his call. Mary Jane Strayer would be delighted to go out with him later tonight. Rand had made up his mind. He was going to the Merlton Library tomorrow to check out its librarian, that mysterious enigma named Jamie Saraceni.

The Merlton Library was in a state of chaos. The volunteer scheduled to read to the group of two- and three-year-olds was stranded on Interstate 295 with a flat tire, leaving the eight children who'd already been dropped off by their grateful mothers for the weekly story hour on the loose in the library.

The "library latchkey kids," the school-age children who came to the library after school and stayed until they were picked up by their mothers after work, arrived in a pack, boisterous and restless from being cooped up all day in their classrooms at Merlton Elementary School. The kids, ranging in age from five to ten, arrived every day because there was no one at home to care for them, and their limited family budgets didn't allow for paid baby-sitters. As there was no inexpensive after-school day care in town, the mothers felt that their children were safer in the library than unsupervised at home or in the streets.

Cindy, the new high-school volunteer, seemed paralyzed by the prospect of returning a cartful of books to the shelves arranged according to the Dewey decimal system. She announced that she couldn't cope with the task and disappeared into the stacks with the library's latest issue of *Rolling Stone*.

Three elderly patrons lined up at the front desk with books to check out.

Jamie Saraceni surveyed the scene and wondered why the library-science curriculum hadn't included a course on crisis management. Fortunately, she'd grown up in the unorthodox bustle and confusion of the Saraceni family; she'd learned to thrive in a three-ring-circus atmosphere.

Jamie's composure never faltered as she routed Cindy from the stacks and pressed her into reading to the toddlers in the activity room. She sent Ashley, a fifth-grader and the oldest library latchkey kid, along for reinforcement. Then Jamie efficiently checked out the books, dispatched the patrons, then herded the young after-school crowd into the research room for a snack of peanut butter cookies and juice.

A remarkably short time later, calm reigned in the library. Jamie took advantage of it to catalogue the shipment of new books that had arrived that afternoon. Standing behind the desk, immersed in her work, she glanced up as she heard another patron approach.

"May I help you?" Her eyes connected with a pair of light brown eyes, an intriguing shade, not quite light enough to be described as golden, but close enough if one exercised a little literary license. Those arresting eyes were alert, intelligent and the most striking feature in a masculine face composed of attractive features.

Her gaze took inventory of them all. The fine straight nose. The firm, well-shaped mouth and strong jaw. The beguiling cleft in the chin. The hair, thick and dark brown in color, slightly overlapped the collar of his well-washed gray Philadelphia Flyers sweatshirt that looked as if it had been owned for a long time and someone had actually sweated in it. Jeans, equally well-worn, fit snugly.

He was very tall, probably six foot three, and his hard, muscular body looked very strong.

Jamie's mouth went dry, and her lashes fluttered involuntarily. The man possessed a virile magnetism and sexual intensity that called forth a primal, feminine response from deep within her. She felt breathless, as if someone had dealt a blow directly to her solar plexus. And more than a little disoriented. Never before had she reacted so physically to a man. A slow heat suffused her body, turning her cheeks pink.

"I—I'm looking for a book," Rand said, and then nearly groaned aloud at his reply. What else did one look for in a library? he silently scorned himself. Smooth, Rand, real smooth.

His mind seemed to have gone blank; his carefully concocted reason for being there totally eluded him. From the moment his eyes met her dark blue gaze, he felt the world tilt on its axis, sending a surge of dizzying heat through his body.

He'd heard women described as knockouts, of course, but this was the first time Rand felt as if he was actually experiencing the phrase. He'd taken one look at this young woman and been knocked out of his senses.

Taken feature by feature, she did not fall into the category of classic beauty. But the way her features were put together—the wide mouth with sensually full lips, the upturned chin and small nose—made one forget the criteria for classical beauty. Her smooth milk-white complexion was an intriguing contrast to her black-as-night hair, which was shiny and soft and almost shoulder length. Her vivid china-blue eyes fringed by dark, thick lashes packed the most potent punch of all.

Rand caught his breath and lowered his gaze to her silky yellow blouse. Beneath it, her breasts were firm and full and looked as if they would fit his hands perfectly. When his imagination dared to ponder their shape and size, he could barely manage to suppress his groan of arousal.

The name pin affixed to her blouse read Jamie Saraceni. She was the librarian! The one who'd turned Daniel Wilcox into an overeager pesky adolescent, panting at the library door. The one who'd resisted the usually suave Daniel's each and every approach. Rand's eyes gleamed, sparked by determination and intrigue. He'd never backed away from a challenge; in fact, far too few challenges seemed to come his way these days. Now he was gazing right at one.

"What book are you looking for?" Jamie asked. She forced herself to look away from him. He was the sexiest man she'd ever seen and she, Jamie Saraceni, who prided herself on her ability to look beyond appearances, whose cool and calm were family legend, was tingling from the sizzling electricity of his masculinity.

The way he was looking at her with that challenging, come-hither glint in his eyes set off alarm bells in her head. He was a charming, cheerfully appalling rogue who broke women's hearts and went on his merry way, unaware of the misery he'd caused because his own heart was impervious to damage. She knew the type and considered herself immune. It was a point of pride with her.

"Perhaps you didn't hear me," she said coolly. Oh, he'd heard, she was certain of that. He was just playing eye contact games, which he played with daunting expertise. Her jaw tightened. "I asked what book you're looking for."

Rand looked down at the stack of books on the desk. On the top of the pile was the latest sex-blood-and-action book by Brick Lawson, the best-selling author adored by the reading public and disdained by each and every serious literary critic.

The true identity of Brick Lawson, a pseudonym, was a guarded secret sometimes speculated upon by magazines and newspapers reporting the latest, ever greater sales of each successive novel. There were rumors that Lawson was a secret agent and the tales were based on his true-life exploits. Only his publisher, editor, agent, family and a few close friends knew that the writer of the hot-blooded books was really the rebel blue blood, Rand Marshall.

Jamie's eyes followed the direction of Rand's gaze. She picked up the newest Brick Lawson release gingerly, handling it as if it were germ-infested. "You're looking for this?" She tried and failed to keep the distaste from her voice.

"You don't approve of Brick Lawson?" Rand asked wryly. There had been so many brickbats flung at the Brick Lawson blockbusters that he'd developed a tough, nearly impenetrable hide concerning them. Great literature they weren't, and he knew it. But he had fun writing them, and Lord, did they sell!

"He's a very popular...writer." She seemed to use the word reluctantly. "I already have a three-page waiting list of people signed up for that book, which is his newest."

Rand decided it best to veer away from the subject of Brick Lawson's newest book. "Since I'm not on the waiting list, I guess I'd better find something else." His eyes locked with hers again. Once again he felt that staggering jolt of electricity that made his body tighten.

This was ridiculous, he chided himself. Brick Lawson wrote about being zapped by sexual chemistry, but that was fiction. Pulp fiction, Jamie Saraceni would undoubtedly add. But here Rand stood in the Merlton Library reacting to the undeniable chemistry arcing between him and the librarian. He was spooked and challenged at the same time.

"What do you personally...enjoy?" he asked, and by the smile on his face and the tone of his voice, it was debatable whether he was talking about reading material.

She shot him a quelling glance, chose another book and proceeded to answer, librarian-to-patron, ignoring his playful innuendo. If that's what it was. "Why not try this one? It's a political espionage thriller, very well-written, with a superbly constructed plot and—"

"You don't think Lawson's *Assignment: Jailbait* is well-written or constructively plotted?"

"Oh, please!" She rolled her eyes heavenward.

"That bad?"

"I admit I haven't read it, but I did hear it compared to that definitive Brick Lawson masterpiece *Land of 1000 Vices*, which I did read. Or tried to." Her big, expressive eyes made any additional comments unnecessary.

"Let me hazard a wild guess," Rand said dryly. "You weren't a *Vice* fan."

"I made the mistake of trying to read it during my lunch hour. I had to throw my sandwich away after the first chapter. The opening scenes, alternating between the seduction in the candy factory and the massacre in the shark tank, nauseated me. Literally."

He probably should take offense, Rand thought. After all, *Land of 1000 Vices* was his most successful book. It had sold thousands in hardcover, an additional million in paperback, and had been made into a successful TV miniseries. He'd received thank-you letters from candy manufacturers crediting him with boosting sales via that opening seduction scene.

And she'd just said it had made her sick.

"Granted, the shark scene was gory, but what did you find objectionable in the candy scene?" he asked with an ingenuousness that was strictly tongue-in-cheek. "The melted chocolate? The tub of marshmallow cream or—"

"The whole thing!" Jamie snapped. He was needling her, and they both knew it. What bothered her most was her volatile response. She was an expert at ignoring teasing, taunts and gibes; she prided herself on frustrating would-be jokesters with her cool, unruffled calm. But not this time. This man seemed to get to her.

"Do you want this book or not?" she asked, determined to repair the slip in her composure.

"Okay, I'll take it." He examined the book she'd recommended. "This author is a darling of the literary critics, but his sales records are nowhere near Brick Lawson's. I suppose you think that's a regrettable commentary on the public's taste?"

He was baiting her again, but this time Jamie refused to nibble. "May I have your library card?"

"Library card?" He hadn't thought of that. But then his purpose for being here was to check out the librarian, not a

book. "I...don't have a card here. I have one from the
Haddonfield Library, though."

"Haddonfield? Is that where you live?"

He nodded. Here it comes, he thought. The then-what-
are-you-doing-in Merlton question. He hadn't bothered to
dream up an answer and he should have. A Haddonfield
resident wouldn't come to Merlton without a very specific
reason. Though the two South Jersey towns were only a few
miles apart geographically, a mammoth chasm separated
them culturally, economically and socially.

Haddonfield was an elegant and well-to-do community
with stately homes on tree-lined streets and a plethora of
trendy little shops offering the latest in upscale merchan-
dise. Real estate was at a premium, because it was exactly
the sort of fashionable place the upper class—and those aspiring to it—wanted to live.

Crowded, run-down, working-class Merlton was its an-
tithesis, a dilapidated, decaying industrial town in decline.
The kind of town the younger inhabitants couldn't wait to
leave and the older ones couldn't afford to leave.

"Not everyone who lives in Haddonfield is a yuppie or a
preppie living on inherited wealth," said Rand, guessing
that she was aware of the town's demographics. "We have
some bona fide members of the traditional middle class living there, too."

Not that he was a member of that group, but instinct told
him that Jamie Saraceni would prefer it if he were.

"We have some of those living in Merlton, too." Jamie's
voice held a slightly defensive edge. "Not everyone in town
is a bookie or a numbers runner."

"Stereotypes." Rand smiled and shrugged. "I guess we're
all guilty of believing in them to some extent. I admit that
until I saw you, I pictured a librarian as a—"

"Don't bother to say it. By denying stereotypes, you're
actually enforcing them," she said dampeningly. "Here, I'll
give you the form to fill out for a library card. Then you can
check out the book."

She stepped back from the desk to open a drawer filled with papers, giving Rand his first opportunity to study her full length. He was quick to take advantage of it.

His gaze swept over her tiny waist, which was accentuated by her wide navy and yellow belt, and lingered appreciatively on the smooth curves of her hips, discreetly revealed by her pencil-slim navy skirt. She was about five foot four, small-boned and slender, but femininely curvaceous in all the right places.

He felt his blood pool and thicken in his groin and swiftly averted his eyes. But looking away proved to be too difficult, and he succumbed to the temptation of studying her legs, which were encased in tinted nylons. Her calves were well-defined and her ankles slender; he imagined her legs would look smashing in a pair of high heels. They were certainly shapely enough in her plain, practical low-heeled shoes.

Jamie turned around just in time to see him staring at her legs. Sexual intent burned in his eyes, and she went very still. He looked hard and dangerous and way out of her league.

A shiver of warning rippled through her. After all, what did she know of him, except that he'd evoked within her the most intense and powerful physical reaction to a man she had ever experienced? And what sort of reliable test of character was that? Hadn't men like Bluebeard also exerted a charismatic effect upon the unfortunate females in their lives?

And for all she knew, he might be married! She didn't even know this man's name!

"Rand Marshall." His voice was deep and low and velvety smooth, a sexy growl that made her heart jump. "I'm thirty-four years old, a graduate of the University of Virginia and am not now and have never been married."

It was as if he'd read her mind! Jamie swallowed and dragged her eyes away from his, feeling tense and edgy. This man was experienced; he knew and understood women far too well.

Rand smiled what he hoped was his most winning, trustworthy smile as he filled out the paper she'd laid on the
desk. He'd seen the apprehension in her eyes when she'd
caught him appraising her and read it for what it was. Now
he had to reassure her that he wasn't the smooth, cocky
heartbreaker she'd already pegged him as.

"I live in Haddonfield but I'm here in Merlton on business," he said chattily, slouching slightly, striving for a body
language that conveyed the message that this was a nice,
wholesome, harmless guy.

He didn't want her wary and on guard. He was too experienced not to know that he'd had the same powerful
physical impact on her as she'd had on him. He studied Jamie covertly, trying to gauge the effects of his trustworthy
smile and reassuring body language.

By the expression on her face, she wasn't buying any of
it.

"You're in Merlton on business?" Her sardonic tone
confirmed that she was extremely skeptical of him and his
motives.

Rand decided that his entire credibility hinged on his alleged business in Merlton. He could hardly mention Daniel
Wilcox, nor was he about to admit to being Brick Lawson.
She'd already made her opinion of his writing quite clear. If
she were to learn that the author of what she considered
nausea-inducing prose was standing before her, he wouldn't
stand a chance with her. She would rebuff him as totally and
determinedly as she had Daniel. Rand was certain of that.

His eyes landed on the sexy cover of *Assignment: Jailbait*. "I'm an insurance claims adjuster," he said, borrow-
ing the occupation of his main character in the book. All the
macho heroes in Brick Lawson's epic adventures had dull,
safe, ordinary jobs, which made their plunge into the world
of sex and danger totally incongruous.

"Today is my day off, but a client here in Merlton called
me unexpectedly, so here I am. Not exactly dressed for success today, am I?"

It sounded plausible, but there was something about the gleam in his eyes. A masculine challenge? A private joke? Jamie wasn't sure but her feminine intuition, alerted by the impact of his virile intensity, warned her to beware.

Rand finished filling out the paper and handed it to her.

"Thank you, Mr. Marshall," she said crisply. "I'll have your card for you in just a few minutes."

"Call me Rand." It was an order, not a request.

She could hardly refuse; this wasn't Victorian England where the use of first names was improper. Still, Jamie wanted to balk at his demand. She knew instinctively that he was a man who was accustomed to being obeyed, one who would try to dominate a woman and with most women probably succeed.

But not with Jamie Saraceni. She'd held her own among the unconventional Saracenis all these years; she wasn't about to mindlessly capitulate to this sexy, strong and exciting...insurance adjuster?

Rand felt his impatience mount. Jamie had an expressive face, and her mental machinations were all too visible to him. She was hesitating, still drawing back. He thought of Daniel's futile three-week campaign to get one date with her and rebelled. But that wasn't going to happen to him. Rand Marshall did not scheme, beg or grovel for a date with any woman.

"Give me your phone number and I'll call you," he said with the authority spawned by unshakable self-confidence. The ingratiating smile and body language were gone, replaced by his usual sexually dangerous, irresistible style.

It had an immediate effect on Jamie. The volatile thrill of excitement shooting through her was staggering in its intensity. Any force capable of rattling her staunch self-control was to be avoided at all cost. "I'd rather not," she said firmly.

He stared at her. "What?"

"I'd rather not give you my phone number. There is really no reason for you to call me."

He was incredulous, not quite comprehending. This had never happened to him before. When Rand Marshall asked for a woman's phone number, she immediately wrote it down for him.

"No reason for me to call?" he repeated. His voice cracked slightly. "How about to talk? Isn't that what phones are for?"

"We have nothing to say to each other."

"Nothing to say?" Confusion, frustration and rage boiled up inside him. "Listen, baby, I have plenty to say to you!" He paused for a moment to collect his scattered thoughts.

Jamie jumped right in. "Then say whatever it is you want to say now because I'm not giving you my phone number."

This he didn't need! He should storm out of the library right now and never come back. He was on the verge of doing exactly that when his gaze accidentally collided with hers. He saw the fire glowing in her eyes, making them even more vivid and beautiful. He looked at her mouth. Her sensuous, full lips were drawn into a pout he found both sultry and arousing. What would that sexy little mouth feel like against his lips?

A shock of heat spread from his abdomen to his chest and went straight to his head. His eyes strayed to her breasts and he watched, hot and hungry, as they rose and fell beneath the soft, silky material of her blouse.

Whatever anger he'd felt was abruptly transformed into something else entirely. He felt stimulated and challenged, the way he did when he was working on an especially interesting plot twist in one of his books. The way he didn't with women whose predictable capitulation to him caused him to quickly lose interest.

"I understand what you're doing," he said silkily, his eyes taunting her with challenge. "You think that playing hard to get will heighten your allure and I'll—"

"I'm not playing hard to get!" Jamie exclaimed. She was indignant at the very suggestion. "I don't want you to—to *get* me, you big, conceited—"

"Ape?" Rand supplied helpfully. "Big conceited ape. Although you could also go with jerk, jackass, creep or fool." They were epithets that Brick Lawson's heroines invariably flung at their leading men, before their eventual, inevitable surrender to the heroes' sexual prowess. "I can come up with more, if you'd like. My mind is a virtual thesaurus."

"I can think up my own insults. I don't need any assistance from you." It was difficult to maintain a stern demeanor when what she really wanted to do was laugh. This was a first, Jamie conceded. She'd never met a stuck-on-himself heartbreaker with a self-deprecatory sense of humor.

Rand saw the laughter she was trying to suppress lurking in her eyes. "Give me your phone number, Jamie," he said smoothly.

Jamie scowled. He'd sensed her momentary weakening and zeroed in on it. He was too quick and far too perceptive. He might be the most sexy, handsome, charming guy to ever come down the New Jersey Turnpike, but oh, she was so right not to let him into her life. "Not in a million years."

He was undaunted. "Jamie, I know why you're trying to hold out. You're afraid of the things I make you feel."

"The things you make me feel are contempt, disdain and—and sheer disbelief at the size of your ego."

"In that order?" Rand laughed. He was enjoying himself. He didn't mind the sparring because he was confident she would give him what he wanted in the end. What woman hadn't? Reaching over the desk, he tore a piece of paper from a notepad, then took a pen from the circular pencil holder. "Here, honey. Write down your number for me."

Jamie gaped at him, amazed by his confidence, persistence and, most of all, by his thick-skinned resistance to rejection. Truly, this was a man who seldom, if ever, had heard the word no from a woman. Her eyes narrowed to slits. He was about to hear it now.

Two

No." Her voice, firm and clear, brooked no argument.

Rand didn't argue, he didn't even attempt to. He genially ignored her refusal. "Okay, then *I'll* write it down." He poised the pen over the paper. "Just give me the first seven digits."

"There are only seven digits in a phone number."

He grinned. "Smart girl. I thought I'd catch you with that one."

She almost smiled back. His cheerful teasing invited one to laugh along with him—and made him far more dangerous than those other smooth operators with their pseudo-sincerity and faux compliments and promises. She had no trouble keeping those sweet-talking smoothies at bay; she'd never been remotely tempted by any of their lures. But with Rand Marshall....

She had to keep her resolve firm. She had to keep reminding herself that he was the kind of man she'd spent her adult years deliberately and successfully rebuffing. So instead of smiling or making any reply at all, she simply ignored him, busying herself with the card file.

Rand heaved an exaggerated sigh. "All right, you win. If you give me your phone number, I'll call you at eight o'clock tonight."

Her eyes widened with incredulity. "Haven't you heard a word I've said?"

"I've heard every word, honey. Which is why I finally caved in and gave you a definite date and time when I'd call. That's what you've been angling for, isn't it?"

"What I've been angling for is for you to leave me alone!"

"I'm not going to let you alone until you give me what I want." His grin was rakish, his eyes gleaming, and Jamie guessed he wasn't talking about a phone number.

"After taking what you want from me, you won't be able to let me alone fast enough," Jamie blurted out. She wasn't talking about phone numbers, either. "Forget it, Rand. I don't want you to call me. I don't want to go out with you. Is there any other way to say it? I don't want to have anything to do with you!"

He was momentarily nonplussed. He was planning his comeback—should he be glib? penitent? masterful?—when a shrill, ear-splitting voice filled the air.

"Miss Saraceni, this little kid just had an accident!"

Before either Jamie or Rand could move, a bright-eyed, grinning girl of about ten trotted over to the desk, holding the hand of an obviously damp story hour patron.

"So it was *that* kind of an accident?" Rand was the first to speak, and he sounded amused.

Jamie envied him his aplomb. Her emotions were still roiling. "What happened, Ashley?"

"Cindy was trying to read *The Three Billy Goats Gruff*, and Mark stood up and yelled 'Go potty.'" Ashley pointed to the little boy and giggled. "But he didn't yell it soon enough. He's soaked! Cindy said she couldn't cope and told me to bring him to you."

Rand chuckled. He was inordinately relieved by the children's interruption. His quest for Jamie's phone number had dead-ended, leaving him uncharacteristically groping for what to do and say next. Now he could postpone his response and regroup his wits before launching his next offensive. *Because he was going to get that phone number.*

He turned his full attention to the two children. "Looks like he could definitely use a change, all right. Where's Mark's mom?"

"She's having an hour of peace and freedom," young Ashley said knowingly. "I heard some of the mothers talking and they said they were so glad that Miss Saraceni started the story hour for the little kids 'cause it gave them at least one hour of peace and freedom a week."

"You mean there's more of these little munchkins here?" asked Rand. "Without their mothers?"

"There's a whole roomful," said Ashley. "And the story hour lady didn't show up and Cindy is doing an awful job reading to them. The kids are starting to run around and jump off their chairs."

Jamie glanced at her watch. "Their mothers won't be here for another thirty-five minutes. That's an eternity in a roomful of running, chair-jumping toddlers. I'd better take over for Cindy and send her out here to work the desk. Hopefully, she'll be able to cope with stamping the checkouts, especially since there usually aren't many at this hour."

Little Mark suddenly raced off, turning to flash Ashley a big, catch-me-if-you-can grin. "He doesn't want to go back to the story group, Miss Saraceni," observed Ashley. "Can I play with him in the kids' corner?"

"I think that would be an excellent idea, Ashley," said Jamie. "First you'd better have him change into these." Jamie opened a desk drawer and produced a pint-sized pair of sweatpants, which she kept around for emergencies like this. "Then you can bring him to the kids' corner." She gestured to the corner of the library, which was set up especially for preschoolers with a child-sized table, wooden blocks and a dollhouse, among other toys. Ashley nodded and escorted Mark away.

"Toys?" Rand said incredulously, staring at the area. "In the library?"

"They're all donated items or things I found at yard sales," explained Jamie. "I wanted a special place with lots of things to do to keep the little kids occupied while their parents browse."

Rand gave his head a disbelieving shake. "You run your library a lot differently from the library in the town where I grew up. Absolutely no noise was permitted there, and the idea of toddlers running around would've given the librarian a cardiac arrest. She was one of—"

"No stereotypes, please." Jamie came from behind the desk. She saw Rand's eyes slide over her and fought to ignore the way the masculine hunger in his eyes made her heart jump.

"You smash the stereotype to smithereens," Rand said softly, falling in step beside her. "Jamie, I—"

He didn't have a chance to finish. A whirlwind in a short denim skirt and jacket came from nowhere to hurl herself between them. "Hi, Jamie, can I borrow your car?" implored a breathless teenage brunette whose thick dark hair was moussed and spritzed to an awesome width. "I *have* to go to the mall."

"You make it sound like a matter of life and death, Saran," said Jamie with what she hoped passed as amused affection. Inwardly, she was groaning. Not her cousin Saran! Not now!

"It is!" insisted Saran. "The black leather skirt I've been wanting is on sale at forty percent off. I have to get there, Jamie. I have to have that skirt."

"Black leather?" Jamie frowned. "Oh, Saran, I don't think—"

"Don't try and talk me out of it," Saran interrupted with a scowl. "I read in a magazine that every woman seriously interested in attracting men should invest in a short black leather skirt and wear it with high heels.''

Rand tried and failed to suppress a laugh.

Saran turned to stare at him. "Who are you?" she demanded, scrutinizing him from head to toe. Although the young woman's eyes were a dark, velvety brown, she looked enough like Jamie for Rand to know at once that they were related.

"His name is Rand Marshall, and he is an insurance claims adjuster," Jamie explained patiently. "This is my cousin, Saran Saraceni," she said to Rand.

"Oh." Saran shrugged, immediately uninterested. "I thought maybe he was that wacko dentist who's after you. What'd he send you today, Jamie?"

Rand's ears perked. "Wacko dentist?" he repeated carefully.

"Yeah. What a dweeb!" Saran shook her head, her voice thick with scorn. "He's been begging Jamie to go out with him since she took Timmy to his office almost a month ago. And you wouldn't believe all the presents he sends to the library almost every day. Balloons and candy and flowers and stuffed animals. Jamie has the latchkey kids play bingo and gives the stuff away as prizes to the winners."

Jamie winced. "Saran, please! That's enough!"

Rand's lips twitched. There was something perversely funny in suave Daniel being viewed as a weirdo whose tokens of affection were raffled off to a bunch of kiddies. "Sounds like you have a dedicated admirer," he drawled.

"Only because I said no to him, and he refused to accept it," Jamie said tightly. "Sound familiar? Anyway, Dr. Wilcox is chiefly dedicated to admiring himself. He's a self-absorbed boy with an undeserved sense of entitlement. I know the type all too well."

"And worst of all, Jamie's friend Angela works in his office and is madly in love with him," Saran added, tossing her long, wild hair.

"That's an interesting twist," Rand said lightly. He wondered if Daniel knew that his hygienist was in love with him and decided he probably didn't. As Jamie had pointed out, Daniel did tend to be self-absorbed.

"The entire situation has been an embarrassment." Jamie looked dismayed. "I'd really rather not discuss it."

"Okay, we'll discuss something else," Saran agreed. Her eyes flicked over Rand and narrowed perceptively. "Are you and Jamie going out?"

"Saran!" hissed Jamie through clenched teeth.

Rand chuckled. "We haven't made a date yet, but I have high hopes. What about Saturday, Jamie?"

"What about tonight?" Saran interjected. "You can go out for dinner and then I won't have to get Jamie's car back here by six so she can drive home. I have lots of shopping to do."

Jamie drew in a sharp breath. The thought of muzzling Saran was infinitely appealing.

"Tonight sounds good to me." Rand smiled. The kid cousin had given them the perfect opportunity to start over, and he grabbed it. "Will you have dinner with me, Jamie?"

"No, I'm sorry, I really can't," said Jamie.

"I know a great new Chinese res—No?" Rand stared at her.

Jamie was shaking her head. "But thank you for the invitation," she added, robotically polite.

No? The word reverberated through Rand's skull. No, again? Frustration began to build within him. He didn't mind playing at romantic strategies for a while, but enough was enough.

"Why not?" he heard himself ask. "Do you have other plans for tonight?"

"Nah, she doesn't have other plans," Saran said, scoffing. "It's just that Jamie won't go out with anybody unless they provide at least two character references and a letter from their clergyman. Doesn't make for a real lively social life, believe me.''

"Saran, I'm going to wring your neck,'' Jamie promised sweetly.

Saran grinned, unrepentant and unalarmed. "If you give me the keys to your car, I'll be out of here and out of your hair."

"You can borrow my car, but you have to have it back here by six, Saran. I need it to drive home.'' Jamie tried to sound firm, but it was clearly a Saran victory. Another one. The young woman had a talent for getting her own way.

Just as Saran made her triumphant departure, Cindy came flying through the doors in a state of high agitation. "Miss Saraceni, I refuse to stay with those little brats for another minute. One of them bit me!'' She held out her arm. "Look at those teeth marks! The little vampire almost drew blood!''

While Jamie attempted to calm Cindy, Rand slipped out the library door. He saw Saran Saraceni opening the door of a meticulously clean silver-gray Honda Civic. "Hey, Saran!''

She looked up and waited as he approached her.

"What kind of name is Saran?'' Rand asked affably. "Did they call you after the plastic wrap or something?''

Saran looked pained, like she'd been asked the question one time too many. "It was supposed to be SaraAnn, all one word, but my folks dropped one A and forgot the extra n on my birth certificate, so it's Saran. If you knew my folks, it makes perfect sense. Any other questions?''

"Just one. Could you be bribed into giving me your cousin Jamie's phone number?''

"Bribed?'' She gasped. "You mean you'd pay me? Like money?''

"Cash.'' Rand smiled. "Maybe you'd like a new shirt to go with that black leather skirt you're going to buy?'' He reached into his wallet and pulled out a twenty-dollar bill.

Her dark eyes widened. Because he was thoroughly enjoying the drama, he took out another ten.

"You'd give me thirty dollars?" squeaked Saran. She extended her hand toward the bills, then drew back. "You're not a hit man or anything like that, are you?" she demanded warily.

Rand suppressed a grin. How refreshing that the woman had some scruples about selling out her cousin. "Word of honor, I'm simply an admirer of your cousin's. Like the dentist," he added dryly.

Saran took the money and recited the phone number while he carefully wrote it down on the inside of his checkbook. "Well, I think you're as crazy as that dentist," she said, tucking the bills into her purse. "You're wasting your money and your time going after Jamie. She'll never go out with you. Once she says no, she means it."

"The irresistible force meets the immovable object," Rand said thoughtfully. "In physics—"

"Physics? Yuck! I'm out of here." Saran completely lost interest in him and the conversation. She hopped into the car and drove away with a jaunty honk of the horn.

Rand returned to the library as the mothers were shepherding their toddlers out the door and down the front steps. Inside, Jamie talked Cindy into overseeing the latchkey kids as they settled in the activity room with scissors, paper and glue.

Jamie glanced at her watch. It seemed an eternity until six o'clock. She felt her energy lagging and considered running up the street to Millie's Diner for a take-out cup of Millie's infamous coffee. It was so strong by this time of day that it was almost like a straight infusion of pure caffeine.

A can of cola suddenly appeared on the desk before her, with a hand attached to it. Her eyes flew to Rand Marshall's face. "You!"

He smiled wryly. "You're glad to see me. I'm convinced I saw it in your eyes for one unguarded second. Here." He shoved the icy can of soda toward her. "This is for you. I thought you could use a pick-me-up. I usually do at this time of day."

She knew she should probably reject his offering. After all, this was a man who needed absolutely no encouragement. But she was too thirsty, and he was right. She did need a liquid pick-me-up. So she opened the can and sipped.

"Did you think I'd gone?" Rand asked conversationally, watching her drink.

"Yes. I thought you'd finally realized that I meant what I said and—"

"Five five five nine seven two five," Rand recited smugly.

Jamie nearly choked. "That's—that's my phone number!" She gaped at him, her blue eyes wide and astonished. "Wh—Where—How—"

"Cousin Saran. Now don't condemn her too hastily. She did ascertain that I wasn't a hit man before she handed it over."

"Oh! Just wait until—"

"Don't be too hard on her, Jamie. I made her an offer she couldn't refuse, so to speak. Saran isn't as implacable and intractable as you are."

Jamie glowered at him. "Saran is seventeen, going on thirty. She hates Merlton and considers school a waste of her time. Her goal in life is to go to New York, become a model and ultimately make the cover of the *Sports Illustrated* swimsuit issue."

Rand shrugged. "She's a striking young woman, if a little on the short side. She might make it." He should know; he'd dated enough models to run an agency.

"Please don't tell Saran that. We're having enough trouble trying to convince her to endure the final two months of high school till graduation."

"We?"

"My parents and I. They're her legal guardians. Her mother is dead, and her father is a relic of the hippie era and is forever backpacking to places like Nepal and Morocco, anywhere but New Jersey. My folks don't mind if she goes to New York after she graduates and turns eighteen. But I think she should further her education and—''

"I'm something of an expert on conflicting goals and family expectations," Rand interrupted. "Let the kid make her own choices, Jamie. You can't expect her to live her life your way. You're two completely different personalities. Boy, are you different!" he added dryly. "Do you really demand character references from a man before you'll have dinner with him?"

"Of course not." Jamie heaved a sigh. "Saran over-exaggerates, overdramatizes and overstates everything." She fixed him with an unyielding stare. "But it's true that I don't go out with strangers."

"And I'm a stranger? But I gave you my vital statistics," he reminded her. "You know more about me than I know about you."

"I'm twenty-five years old, have a degree in library science and am not now nor have I ever been married." She followed his lead from his own glib biography.

"And you get your kicks giving men a hard time," he added.

"That's not true!"

"Sure it is. You guard your phone number like it's a classified document, although I assume you occasionally give it to some noble candidate you deem worthy enough to speak with over the phone. So what comes next in this fixed screening agenda of yours? You talk on the phone to the poor schlemiel and then—''

"After a few telephone conversations, if they go well, I might agree to meet the *person* for lunch," Jamie said, frowning. She glared at him. "Why am I telling you this? Why am I bothering to talk to you at all?"

"Are those rhetorical questions or do you want an answer?"

"I don't think I'd care to hear any answer you'd come up with."

"No, you probably wouldn't." Rand laughed. "But I'm going to tell you anyway. You're talking to me because you want me to hang around. You're attracted to me, Miss Saraceni. I turn you on, I won't take no for an answer, and you're intrigued, in spite of yourself."

She flushed hotly. "Oh, you really are a conceited ape, jerk, jackass—" What were those other insults he'd suggested earlier? She was too flustered to remember.

"Right on cue." Rand smiled, thinking of every sexy scene he'd ever written. "Now it's my turn to tell you how gorgeous you are when you're angry. How hot and fiery and sexy." He moved with agile grace around the corner of the desk to join her behind it.

He was much too near. Wasn't there an old song with lyrics portending the dangers of being too close for comfort? Jamie felt as if she was living them. She took a deep, steadying breath. "You're not allowed back here. It's against the rules for anyone but library personnel."

"And you always follow the rules, don't you, Miss Jamie?" Rand taunted. He reached out to trace the fine line of her jaw from her ear to her chin.

Jamie jumped away as if she'd been scalded. "Yes, I do. Rules are made to be followed."

Rand's laugh was low and sexy. "You've set me up, baby. You know I have to contradict you on that one. I think you secretly want me to." He took several steps, nearly sandwiching her between himself and the back of the desk. "I'll bet there are rules against the librarian on duty kissing a patron, too. But rules are made to be broken."

Her heart was hammering against her ribs, her head was spinning, but she managed to slip away. He looked amused, leaving her to wonder if he'd deliberately chosen to let her escape. Her face was flushed, and the blood roared in her ears. Would he have kissed her? Did she want him to?

"If you don't get out of here right now—" she began. To her horror, her voice was husky and thick and not at all commanding.

He cast her another amused glance before sauntering around the long curved desk back to the patrons' side. "Comfortable now? You're behind the desk, and I'm not. We're not breaking any of your infallible rules."

How did he manage to sound mocking and seductive at the same time? Jamie wondered, striving to regain her usually unflappable composure. No one had ever made her feel this way before, hot and cold, infuriated and giddy, all at the same time! She had to get away from him.

"If you'll excuse me, I'm going to check on Cindy and the children," she said coolly, inclining her chin to an imperious angle as she left the desk to head for the activity room.

"You're not excused." Rand's big hand closed over her wrist like a manacle, chaining her to the spot. "You haven't told me what happens on that big lunch date. You know, when you meet the wimp who finally manages to pass your rigid telephone test. I'm not about to leave with that cliffhanger unresolved."

She drew her lips together into a taut, straight line. "Let go of my wrist."

"Will you finish the story?"

"Only if you'll let me go this minute!" she snapped. Her skin was hot and tingled where he touched her. "And promise to leave immediately afterward!" When Rand let go of her wrist, she unconsciously rubbed it. Jamie swallowed. At this point, she knew she would tell him anything he wanted to know, just to make him go.

She cleared her throat. "To set the record straight, I don't date wimps. The men I've dated have all been sensitive gentlemen."

"Undoubtedly, in the worst sense of the word." Rand snickered. "I'll bet they conduct seminars on their feelings and can cry on cue."

She shot him an icy look of disapproval. "Do you want me to continue?"

"Oh, definitely. I wouldn't miss this for the world."

"Well, after I've agreed to meet the *gentleman* for lunch, we set up the time and place and then arrive and depart in separate cars."

"But of course," said Rand. He flashed a sardonic grin. "Tell me, how many lunches with separate arrivals and departures before you get around to something as daring and risqué as a dinner date? At night! And—" he simulated a scandalized gasp "—in the same car?"

Jamie stiffened. "It's long past the time for you to leave, *Mr. Marshall*. I don't have the time or the inclination to stand here and listen to you make fun of me."

Rand laughed. "Lady, I don't think you know the meaning of the word fun. You wouldn't recognize it in any way, shape or form."

With an indignant sniff, her head held high, Jamie stalked away from him.

At least, she tried to. Rand reached out and caught her by her upper arm, effectively halting her once more. "Now it's my turn. I get to tell you exactly what I think of your doctrine of dating," he drawled.

"I don't want to hear it." She struggled to escape, but she couldn't break free. The power of his masculine strength was affirmed by the fact that he was holding her with only one hand.

"It's the most ridiculous thing I've ever heard," Rand continued, ignoring her protests, both verbal and physical. "Even for an outdated, incorrect stereotype of a librarian, it's rigid and repressive." He grimaced wryly. "Next to you, insurance adjusters are wild party boys living life in the fast lane."

"I don't care what you think," she said coldly. She'd stopped struggling in an effort to preserve her dignity and stood still, taut with tension. "My system works well for me."

"Were you ever assaulted by a man?" he asked, his voice suddenly filled with concern. "Is that why you feel the need to—"

"No, I've never been assaulted," Jamie cut in sharply. "And I never intend to be, either. I simply like to control—"

"You're a control freak, all right. A relationship with you would be similar to life in Stalinist Russia."

Her eyes narrowed to glittering blue slits. "I suppose you think a woman should run around in—in short black leather skirts and high heels and go chasing after any man who crooks his little finger!"

"That's one end of the scale. You're at the other, putting your hapless admirers through the paces, cracking the whip, dangling the carrot, pulling the strings—"

"Do you know any more clichés?" snapped Jamie. "Why not add them to the list?"

"Sure." A feral smile curved his lips. His slightly-too-dark-to-be-golden eyes held a challenging glint. "Here's the most clichéd cliché of them all. The bickering would-be lovers in a hot clinch."

And before Jamie could speak, move or even breathe, he yanked her into his arms. Pressed tightly against him, she could feel the burgeoning strength of him, every taut line of him.

For a split second she was too shocked to struggle. And then the words came all at once, rushing from her in a breathless torrent. "I don't find your Neanderthal tactics amusing in the least, Rand Marshall. I've tried to be a good sport, but now you've gone too far. Let me go this instant or—"

"You'll scream?" Rand asked with interest. He lowered his head and brushed her lips lightly with his. "You can't, it's a library, remember?"

His hands moved audaciously over her, molding her even closer to his strong, male frame. Jamie fought the syrupy warmth that crept through her, making her limbs tremulous and her mind fuzzy. "I'll scream so loudly I'll have the Merlton police here within minutes," she insisted. She felt dizzy and weak, but she denied the overwhelming urge to cling to Rand for support.

"Mmm, will you?" He nibbled sensuously on her earlobe while his big hands smoothed over her back with long, sweeping strokes.

"I'll press charges." Her eyelids were getting heavy, and she had to fight to snap them open. She wanted to relax against his masculine warmth and revel in his strength. Cheeks scarlet with shame, she silently admitted that she wanted his hands to keep caressing her until...until....

By a sheer act of will, she pulled herself together and jerked backward. He was still holding her, but she'd gained enough leverage to pull back and glare up at him. "I know almost all the cops on the force. They'll throw you in jail."

"They'll have to charge me with something first," Rand murmured softly, smiling down at her, not at all concerned with her threats. He began nibbling again, this time on her neck. "What'll it be?"

Jamie whimpered. A thick, hot river of sensation bubbled through her, but she determinedly struggled against it. "Sexual harassment." She wriggled against him in another effort to break loose. He didn't loosen his grip, but her movements electrified them both. Reflexively, Jamie moved again, in order to free herself, but unconsciously, involuntarily, she moved more sinuously this time.

It was a major mistake. Rand made a strange sound that was a combination of a laugh and a groan. "I think it would be damn hard to figure out who's sexually harassing whom at this point, Jamie." His voice deepened and thickened. "Jamie." His mouth hovered seductively, hungrily over hers.

"No," she protested weakly. Though her mind commanded her to push him away, her body refused to accept the order.

"Yes," he breathed. "Oh yes."

His mouth opened over hers and he kissed her, hard.

She wasn't prepared for the stunning surge of need that swept through her as his arms more tightly enfolded her. He was so big and strong; his masculinity evoked a powerful feminine response, the force of which she'd never before experienced. Her eyes fluttered shut, and she gave up the fight and slowly slid her arms around his neck to bring her body even more fully against his.

His mouth was ardent and hungry as it moved over hers. Of their own volition, her lips parted for him, and when he thrust his tongue into her mouth, she made a small, soft sound and gave in to his delicious, erotic demands. Her tongue reached for his, and they rubbed sensuously, tasting, probing, stroking.

A glowing heat blossomed deep in her belly, a secret swelling throb that ached for his touch. And the kiss went on and on, growing deeper and hotter and hungrier. There was nothing in the world but Rand, dominating her mind and body with his passion and his voracious male need. Clinging to him, writhing sensuously in his arms, Jamie felt a pleasure so intense that it bordered exquisitely on pain.

Her mind, always so ordered and controlled, splintered and spun away. For the first time in her life her senses took over, and they were filled with Rand, with the intoxicating taste, touch and scent of him.

Then, abruptly, incredibly, it was over. Rand ended the kiss and pulled away from her.

He stared at Jamie, his eyes dark and intense, his body hard as stone. He felt as if the top of his head had been blown off, a phenomenon often experienced by Brick Lawson's characters, but one their creator, Rand Marshall, never had experienced before. Not cool Rand Marshall, the master of his passion, the smooth operator whose emotions had always remained comfortably detached from his superb technique.

Until now. Somehow sexual desire had combined with emotion to explode into a passionate conflagration. He'd never been so stirred by a single kiss. And they were in a library, of all places, hardly a setting noted for its romantic ambience. But she'd been so passionate and responsive in his arms that he'd quickly reached the point where kissing wasn't enough.

If he hadn't torn himself away from her when he did, he would've pulled her blouse from inside her wide belt and unbuttoned it. And then he would have put his mouth over her nipples, which were so hard and tight that he'd felt their small pressure against his chest when he held her....

A sharp shudder of desire racked him, and he focused his gaze on her lips, which were rosy and wet and slightly swollen.

Jamie stared back at him. The heady taste of him lingered on her lips and her tongue. Her breasts were achy and swollen, the tips tingling and acutely sensitive. There was a warm, provocative moisture between her thighs. She stood there, caught in his gaze, her breathing erratic, her face flushed.

She wanted him. Her body vibrated with urgency. When he looked at her, it was as if he was physically touching her again. She felt a soft thrust of sensation in her already taut nipples as they grew more pointed beneath her clothes. Sharp sensual spears pierced the hot, secret core of her. She was rocked by ambivalence, wanting to press herself tightly, wantonly against Rand as much as she wanted to flee from the sexual danger he presented.

She felt confused and off balance. Never in her twenty-five careful years had she experienced this elemental and profound need to merge with a man. To claim him for herself, to belong to him completely.

It was unnerving, it was insane. Cool, calm Jamie Saraceni wasn't the type to lose her head over a man's kiss. But she had this time; there was no denying it. She was horrified.

"You have to leave," she said in a breathless, husky voice, which she hardly recognized as her own.

"Now I know your secret." Rand's mouth curved into a slow, sexy smile. "The lady librarian isn't controlled and repressed, after all." He sounded inordinately pleased with his discovery. They were going to be dynamite in bed together.

A fierce surge of anger swept through her. She felt exposed and vulnerable, a new experience for her, and she didn't like it one bit. That smug male smile of his and the teasing lilt in his voice were the figurative equivalent of tossing a lighted match into a pool of gasoline. Her fury flamed to flash point. "Get out of here, Rand Marshall. I'm aghast at what happened!"

Rand's laugh was sexy and deep. "Honey, you're hot and bothered because of what happened."

Her whole body was one hot blush. For him to know, to tease her about it. She was mortified.

"I'll leave now, Jamie." His tone made it plain that he was leaving because he wanted to, not because she'd told him to. "And I'll call you," he tossed over his shoulder as he headed for the door.

"I won't talk to you," she called after him.

"Yes, you will," he replied amiably.

She wouldn't, she insisted to herself. The lost continent of Atlantis would reemerge from the sea, a UFO would land on the White House lawn, and New Jersey would secede from the Union before Jamie Saraceni consented to speak to Rand Marshall again.

Three

Every time the phone rang that evening, Jamie jumped. There were calls for her nephews, eight-year-old Brandon and seven-year-old Timmy, for her father, Al, for her mother, Maureen, for her grandmother, and at least five calls for Saran.

There were no calls for Jamie or her sister Cassie, the divorced mother of the boys. Cassie sat in front of the television set—in the Saraceni household, the TV was on from *News at Sunrise* to the end of *The David Letterman Show*—engrossed in a program, oblivious to her lack of calls.

Jamie wished she was. She felt restless and on edge. Not that she wanted Rand Marshall to call, she assured herself. There was only one telephone in the house, in the always occupied kitchen, so privacy during a phone call was unheard of among the Saracenis, and if Rand was to start in with sexually charged innuendos...

"Honey, you're hot and bothered because of what happened." His voice echoed in her head, complete with his rakish laughter. She thought of that rapacious kiss in the library, and her pulses quickened. A sensuous little shiver tingled along her spine.

Even sitting here in the kitchen, surrounded by tax forms—she did the family's taxes every year and April fifteenth was only a month away—Jamie could still feel that stunning shock of sexual awareness that had flashed through her at her first sight of Rand Marshall.

She stared absently into space, reliving that moment. She didn't see the two big cats, a black tom and a gray Persian, coming until they'd leaped onto the table, one after the other, and began a spirited wrestling match. The year's worth of receipts, old checkbooks, credit card slips and tax information returns that Jamie had arranged in neat little piles went flying. A cross-eyed Siamese cat with a well-documented predilection for chewing paper chose that moment to leap onto a tax form that had fallen to the floor.

Jamie groaned in frustration. She was not a cat fancier, which was a definite drawback in a house with seven cats. Sensing that she was not enchanted with their presence, the two furry wrestlers resumed their match under the table, and the Siamese escaped with the tax form between his teeth.

With Jamie hot on his trail, he streaked to one of the upstairs bedrooms and disappeared under a bed. When she heard the unmistakable sound of paper tearing, she conceded defeat and returned to the kitchen muttering, her eyes smoldering as she surveyed the year's worth of income and spending information, which she'd spent hours sorting, scattered all over the floor.

"Jamie doesn't like cats much," Grandma Saraceni observed to no one in particular. "I trace it back to the time she was seven, when Tiger—remember him?—ate her parakeet."

"Gross!" enthused Timmy, looking up from the video game he and his brother were playing. The Saracenis had two television sets in their family room, one for watching, the other hooked up to the children's electronic game system. Both were continually in use.

"I bet there was blood and feathers everywhere!" Brandon added with relish.

"We had a funeral, remember, Jamie?" Grandma said with a smile of reminiscence. "We put the remains—and there sure wasn't much left of that bird—in a shoe box and sang 'Amazing Grace' and 'Battle Hymn of the Republic' before we buried him in the garden."

"I remember, Grandma, it was lovely," said Jamie, stooping to gather the papers.

"Did that nice young dentist drop by the library with any more gifts today, dear?" asked Jamie's mother, glancing up from the doll's hair she was combing. As children, neither bookworm Jamie nor tomboy Cassie had liked dolls, so their mother had taken to collecting them herself. Today, she had over three thousand of them, dolls from the sixties, seventies and eighties, crammed into every available space in the house. She bought, sold and traded them to fellow collectors all over the country.

"He isn't a nice young dentist, Mom, he's a jerk," said Jamie. *Jackass, creep, fool.* She could hear Rand's voice echo in her head and she almost smiled. "And I didn't hear from him today. Hopefully, he finally realized that I have no intention of ever going out with him."

"Nice young dentists don't grow on trees, honey," observed Maureen, dressing the doll in a shimmering black strapless sheath. "Some lucky girl is sure to snap him up."

"Mom, Angela's madly in love with him," Jamie said patiently. "Even if Daniel Wilcox wasn't a jerk, which he most definitely is, I couldn't go out with him without hurting her."

"You're a wonderfully loyal friend, Jamie." Maureen glanced from the doll she held in her hand to her daughter. "And I know that someday soon you're going to meet just the right man for you."

"Maybe she's already met him," Saran piped up. Her big brown eyes widened guilelessly. "Maybe he's that hunk who was coming on to her in the library this afternoon, Rand Something. He's cute enough to be on TV, even if he is an insurance salesman."

"Claims adjuster," Jamie corrected automatically, shooting Saran a look of cousinly reproof. She hadn't forgotten that the little rat had given her phone number to Rand Marshall. She took a deep breath and braced herself for the barrage of comments that was sure to follow.

"Handsome enough to be on TV?" Her mother looked pleased. "Tell us more, Jamie."

"Handsome is as handsome does," said Grandma tartly. "There have been more handsome murderers than I'd care to count, getting by on their looks to hide their fiendish natures."

"Maybe I'd better look through your crime magazines and see if I recognize him in any mug shots, Grandma," Jamie said dryly. Her grandmother, a crime buff since the St. Valentine's Day massacre in underworld Chicago, considered everyone guilty until proven innocent.

"I did it! I found a Warp Zone and it took me to World Four!" bellowed Brandon exultantly, talking in the incomprehensible electronic game jargon that all kids these days seemed to understand. He and Timmy jubilantly slapped each other's palms in a high five.

A white cat and a red-striped one bolted through the room, chased by the big black tom. They ran right through the bowl of popcorn, sitting on the floor between the boys, overturning it. Popcorn went everywhere.

The subject of Rand Marshall was dropped as everybody sprang into action, scolding the cats and sweeping up the popcorn. Jamie was relieved. For reasons she didn't care to examine too closely, she was singularly unwilling to discuss Rand with anyone.

Her uncharacteristic reticence puzzled her. She'd never hesitated to share information about her other hapless pursuers. She knew that some considered it odd that a self-supporting twenty-five-year-old career woman still chose to live at home with her family, but it was her own choice. She liked the involvement and the company. The thought of returning each day to an empty apartment, relentlessly neat and quiet as a tomb, held no appeal for her.

For a moment, she allowed herself to fantasize about coming home to the imaginary cozy home she shared with her imaginary husband. She pictured the charming country kitchen where they would cook dinner together while sharing the details of their day. She visualized the lovely old-fashioned bedroom with the cushioned window seat, the canopied bed with lots of pillows and thick down comforter, a fire crackling in the fireplace. Her husband would love to read in bed, just like she did, and they would lie there side by side, propped up on the pillows, engrossed in their books until their eyes met. And then they would smile and close their books and reach for one another....

Jamie suppressed a sigh of longing. She was careful to keep her fervid romantic streak a well-hidden secret. Her family and friends saw her as methodical, prosaic Jamie who ran her life the way she filed the books in the library. Orderly and precise. She knew her parents were eager for her to find a nice young man to marry in a big, beautiful white wedding; she wanted that, too.

But there could be no love and no wedding until she found a man she could fully trust. Without honesty and trust, a relationship was temporary and meaningless, like her older brother Steve's string of affairs, like her sister Cassie's disastrous marriage to that lying cheat, Wayne Blair.

Observing her brother and former brother-in-law through the years had given Jamie a sort of sixth sense for spotting those charming, self-centered users, cynical and spoiled by the parade of women who kept falling in love with their good looks and smooth lines.

They didn't interest her in the slightest. She was searching for a man who wanted emotional involvement along with the physical intimacy, a man who wasn't merely seeking sexual pleasure without making a commitment and an emotional investment in the woman he took to his bed. The man of her dreams would have a sense of humor so they could laugh together, he would share her values of marriage and family, and he would love her as much as she loved him.

He had to exist. She'd been waiting for him all her life.

When an image of Rand Marshall flashed before her mind's eye, she tried to firmly erase it. How dare he invade her tender, private thoughts of her dream man. It was practically sacrilegious. Rand Marshall was trouble; everything she wanted to avoid. He was even worse than Daniel Wilcox and the other insincere charmers who'd attempted to weasel their way into her life in the past. At least they'd never dared to touch her, while Rand Marshall hadn't hesitated to grab her, to caress her, to kiss her....

Desire, swift and sharp and hot, shuddered through her. The searing heat scorching her made her feel feverish and achy all over again, just the way she'd felt in Rand's arms. Frowning, she remembered how he'd laughed that wicked laugh of his and taunted her about rules being made to be broken. She remembered her loss of control in his arms.

Jamie shivered. He was the most dangerous man she'd ever met. He tempted her, he made her feel things, do things, want things.

Jamie steeled herself against the hot tides flowing through her. She wasn't going to have anything more to do with Rand Marshall, she vowed. Though he would never know it, he was the one man she'd ever met who made her want to break all her own rules.

Rain pounded against the windshield of the Jaguar Vandenplas XJ6 parked in front of the Merlton Library. It was Rand's newest car, his current pride and joy, which he pampered like a pedigreed pet. If anyone had told him three days ago that he'd drive his imported ebony-black beauty to

Merlton, of all places, and in a downpour rivaling the one Noah had endured, Rand would have dismissed them as crazy.

But his body was burning with memories of yesterday's encounter with Jamie Saraceni. He remembered the soft pressure of Jamie's body against his, the hot passion of their kiss, as well as the alert intelligence shining in her eyes and the appealing warmth of her smile. He couldn't stop thinking about her, nor could he ignore the emotions his thoughts evoked.

This was so unlike him, he thought grimly. Rand Marshall, aka Brick Lawson, was accustomed to controlling his thoughts the way he controlled his characters' destinies. He'd always been able to keep his mind aloof from his emotions, in his dealings with his family, in his dealings with women. It was so much easier that way.

In fact, he'd decided long ago that sex was more enjoyable without the threatening entanglements provided by that emotional high some liked to refer to as love. But last night, though he'd been feeling restless and frustrated, he hadn't sought a willing partner to ease those tensions.

Instead, he'd endured them because Jamie Saraceni was so deeply entrenched in his thoughts that he knew it would be impossible to find satisfaction with anyone else.

He mentally implored some unseen deity for help. He'd been living his life comfortably as a self-centered loner; he had no desire to change things right now. Finding himself actively caring about Jamie was terrifying.

Rand grimaced. There was only one way to handle the situation, he decided. He'd have to take Jamie to bed and satiate himself with her. Then put her out of his mind. Once they were in bed together, he'd find out that she was just like the other women he'd taken and forgotten.

But what if she wasn't? taunted that persistent observer who lived in his head. What if having her made him want her more, not less?

Nerves jangling, Rand attempted to calm himself. Stop thinking in long-range terms; you're not used to it, you're not good at it, he reminded himself. Even when he wrote, it was chapter by chapter, much to the chagrin of his editors who would have liked to have an inkling of what was going to happen in the story. But how did he know what was going to occur in chapter ten when he was only on page three?

And that's about where he was with Jamie Saraceni. Page three. And it was time to move on to page four. Flinging open the car door, he dashed through the cold, driving rain toward the wide glass doors of the library.

Jamie handed an orange to each of the library latchkey kids gathered in the Merlton Library activity room. She had unofficially appropriated the room when she'd put together this unofficial after-school program for her unofficial charges. A local women's club generously arranged to donate a fixed sum for daily snacks for the children, which Jamie was responsible for buying and serving.

"Tell Miss Saraceni about the kitten, Scotty," one little boy urged another.

Jamie smiled encouragingly at him. "Do you have a new kitten at home, Scotty?" she asked.

Scotty shook his head. "But I saw this big boy stuffing a kitten in the library book box today."

Jamie's eyes widened. "In the book deposit box?" she repeated incredulously.

The box, located in front of the library, was an old mailbox, which had been removed from use by the local post office and given to the library. It was painted orange and had a sign proclaiming Books Only, Not a Mailbox, but people were forever mailing letters in it anyway. "Someone put a kitten in it?" Letters, yes. A cat was definitely a first.

"Aw, that's just one of Scotty's stupid tall tales," scoffed an older child. "Don't believe him, Miss Saraceni."

Scotty did have a habit of embellishing the truth somewhat, Jamie knew. "But if there really is a kitten in the book drop it could be hurt if some heavy books are dropped on it." She frowned at the notion. She would never call herself a cat lover but she did live with seven of them and felt some loyalty to the species. "It could be hungry."

"Or it could pee on the library books in the box," an enthusiastic kindergartner chimed in.

All the children except Scotty laughed. "I'm not telling a tall tale, Miss Saraceni," he said solemnly. "I *saw* that kitten get put in there."

What choice did she have but to look for the cat? Jamie asked herself as she trudged out to the book deposit box. It was raining, hard enough to require an umbrella, which she held with one hand while studying her key ring, trying to pick out the correct key to open the box.

"May I be of some assistance?" inquired a deep male voice.

Jamie whirled around so fast that she nearly lost her balance. She managed to maintain it, but dropped the key ring into a puddle on the sidewalk. "Rand." Her voice sounded breathless. Her mind plummeted into a morass of chaos and confusion. She wanted to run away, she wanted to stay.

"Mind if I share your umbrella?" he asked and moved closer to stand under it, without waiting for her answer.

The elusive, enticing scent of her perfume wafted into his nostrils, and desire knifed through him. Gingerly, Rand stooped and fished the keys out of the puddle. "I'm looking for a certain book," he said, placing the keys in her palm.

His hand was strong and warm and almost completely covered her own smaller hand. Jamie quivered with involuntary pleasure at the masculine feel of it surrounding hers.

Rand, too, was deeply affected by this simple touching of hands. Shaken, he drew a deep breath and cleared his throat, trying to regroup his defenses. "I've tried the libraries in Haddonfield and Cherry Hill, and neither has it. I thought I may as well try Merlton."

"If the Cherry Hill Library doesn't have the book, chances are great that we won't," Jamie said, striving for a businesslike tone. "It's the Cadillac of libraries while Merlton is the—" She paused, trying to come up with a suitable car metaphor. Her mind wasn't working as keenly as it should.

"Yugo?" suggested Rand.

"Unfortunately, yes." He laughed and Jamie stared at him, she couldn't help herself. She liked the deep rich sound of his laughter and the way his eyes crinkled when he smiled. She liked it way too much.

Remembering last night's solemn vow to keep away from him, she desperately tried to return to the subject of library books. "What's the name of the book you're looking for?" she asked, her voice husky. She didn't sound a bit like her usual crisp, professional self.

"The name of the book," repeated Rand. What was that old adage about the tangled web and practicing to deceive? He should've practiced harder. Well, there were many approaches, and if one failed, the creative contender came up with another.

"I'll be honest, Jamie, I'm not looking for a book." Honesty could sometimes backfire and he didn't often resort to it, but this time he decided to risk it. "The only reason I came here was to see you again."

The exhilaration that surged through her made her feel giddy and excited. Jamie fought against it, trying to recall every reason she shouldn't let Rand Marshall into her life. The problem was, they all seemed hazy and unreal in the vital force of his presence. Nevertheless, she persevered. "Rand, this is impossible."

"Tell me about it." He gave a slight laugh. "I don't make a practice of hanging out in front of libraries. But knowing you were here, I couldn't stay away. All I've been able to think about is you from the moment we met."

"Reel it in," she said shakily. "I'm not about to fall for that old line."

"Line? You think that's a line?" He was indignant. "It happens to be the truth. That's why it isn't working. When I want to spin a woman a line, I make damn sure it's a seductive and irresistible one. If I were feeding you a line, you'd be biting, baby. And I'd be reeling *you* in!"

His outrage struck her as funny. Jamie laughed. "I've never met anyone with an ego as grandiose as yours."

"Your ego is no small thing, either. You think you're the cutest little trick in shoe leather."

"The cutest little trick in shoe leather?" Jamie hooted gleefully. "That's straight out of the nineties, the *eighteen* nineties. If your seductive and irresistible lines are on a par with that, then the women who've been falling for them have IQs in the single digits."

The rain continued to beat against the umbrella, but both were oblivious to it. Rand stared at Jamie, watching her thick, dark shiny hair swing around her neck as she tilted her head. The suit she was wearing was feminine and understated and subtly sexy, hinting at the tempting curves of her figure without actually revealing them.

He gazed into her laughing, taunting eyes, and she met his gaze steadily. Challengingly.

A flash of heat rippled through him. He had to have her. "You're used to calling all the shots, aren't you?" he drawled lazily. "Those poor suckers you bless with your phone number and approved lunch dates really don't stand a chance with you at all."

"And those poor dimwits who fall for your smooth-operator act don't stand a chance with you, either," she retorted.

"It's not an act. I am a smooth operator. One of the smoothest."

"To be forewarned is to be forearmed, I suppose. But I really don't need to worry." Common sense told her to stop this at once. The atmosphere was becoming too sexually charged; the tension between them was tangible and pulsing with sexual excitement. She was deliberately baiting him, pushing him....

But she couldn't seem to stop herself. Challenging him was exhilarating, and though she'd lived quite calmly without exhilaration for the past twenty-five years, it was suddenly too enthralling to give up. "I'm completely immune to you and others of your ilk," she added in a mocking tone that invited retaliation.

His lips curved into a slow, sexy smile. "Maybe you're immune to others of my ilk, but you're far from immune to me. We proved that yesterday." He cupped her shoulders with his hands and slowly drew her toward him. "But I think you want me to prove it again."

"I do not!" But tendrils of heat were uncurling in her abdomen, growing hotter and tighter as his eyes held hers.

"I was honest with you," he said huskily, as he slowly lowered his head to hers. "Despite your mockery and your accusations, I was being honest when I told you that I can't stop thinking about you. You owe me the same honesty, Jamie." Coaxingly, he traced the contour of her upper lip with the tip of his tongue. "Tell me you want this. Admit it to yourself, Jamie. And to me."

Jamie almost moaned. She wanted to seize his head in her hands and press her mouth hotly against his. "No," she whispered, hanging on to the last shreds of her willpower.

"You're the most stubborn woman I've ever met," he murmured, biting gently at her mouth. "You're as strong-willed as I am." The revelation astonished him.

"And you admire me for it." His breath was warm against her lips, and the scent of him, a heady combination of soap and spicy after-shave and musky male, filled her nostrils. Pleasure shuddered through her.

"I don't!" he insisted. He cupped her hips with his hands and lifted her higher and harder against him. "I like women who are compliant and—and...." His voice trailed off, and he drew in a ragged breath.

"Simpleminded?" Jamie suggested. Her hands were on his chest, and when he began to kiss her neck again she reflexively, unthinkingly, uninhibitedly arched her throat to give him greater access, even as she protested, "Rand, don't. We can't. We shouldn't."

"We can, we should and we're going to."

Four

———

His mouth came down on hers, hot and hard and hungry. A wild sound vibrated in her throat, and her lips parted for the bold, insistent thrust of his tongue. Shuddering with hunger and need, Jamie's body melted against his muscular frame. Slowly, her arms glided to his shoulders then curled around his neck in feminine submission.

The stem of the umbrella slid between them, causing the bell-shaped shade to come to rest on top of their heads. Neither noticed. They were kissing deeply, his hands moving over her soft curves, caressing, arousing, learning her as she clung to him, weak with wanting.

Her breasts swelled and pressed against the solid strength of his chest. He attempted to thrust his thigh between her legs, but her straight skirt presented a barrier, keeping him from achieving the intimate posture he sought. A growl of frustration escaped from his throat, a primitive mating sound, low and deep and male. Jamie quivered in response.

Hotly, impetuously, Rand pushed up her skirt with a deft sweep of his hands. Then he slid his leg between hers, molding her to him, his fingers sure and experienced, stroking her bottom, her thighs...

Jamie felt the heat and pressure of his provocative caresses and moaned with helpless pleasure. A hot glowing ache radiated from the very core of her, and her whole body throbbed with the piercingly exquisite sensations. Operating on pure instinct, she began to rotate her hips in a subtle erotic rhythm. All sense of time and place was obliterated by the passion raging through her.

The kiss became wilder and deeper and hungrier. It wasn't until oxygen deprivation threatened that, breathless, they finally broke apart.

Feeling disoriented, Jamie stepped back, but she couldn't tear her gaze from Rand's face. His eyes were dilated and heavy-lidded with passion, and his mouth was moist from kissing her. She felt her skirt slide slowly down her legs to its correct length and suddenly full awareness of what they had been doing, what she must have looked like, *right here in front of the library*, struck her with stunning force.

Her incendiary response to him scared her. He had taken her into his arms, and she'd become a wild thing, sensual and free, governed by the intensity of her emotions. And ungoverned by a whit of sense or propriety.

Tightly clutching the umbrella's handle, she raised it over her head and squeezed back sudden hot tears of mortification. "If someone had seen us..."

She swallowed hard, picturing herself as she had been, wrapped around Rand Marshall, her skirt hiked high, her eyes tightly closed and her mouth open and hungry. She was appalled by her wanton abandon. "I could lose my job, behaving like that."

Rand stared at her, feeling dazed and disconcerted. From the moment he touched her, he'd lost control. Even now, he was having difficulty pulling himself together.

His eyes shifted to the rounded softness of her breasts. He remembered how good they'd felt crushed against his chest, and his breath caught raggedly in his throat. He wanted to see them, to cup them in his hands, to taste them. His blood pulsed hotly and heavily, making him grow harder and tighter with every heartbeat.

He felt wired, his whole body an aching force of desire and need. He couldn't remember the last time a woman had turned him on so fast and so hard, unless it was yesterday when he'd kissed Jamie Saraceni for the first time.

A blast of wind pelted rain in his face, and Rand welcomed it, for the cold air and water helped to clear his head. "Jamie, I don't know what to say." His voice was gravelly with lingering traces of passion. "You're right, the time, the place is all wrong. It's just that when you—when I—" He broke off in confusion. Where was his penchant for dialogue when he really needed it?

It helped that Rand seemed as unhinged by their behavior as she did. Pulling herself together was a conscious act of will but Jamie made herself do it. The icy splash of the raindrops helped. She glanced around, relieved to see that they'd had no witnesses.

"We're safe, I think," she murmured. "There's nobody around." She shivered. "I guess we have the weather to thank for that. No one in his right mind would be out in this."

How true, thought Rand. It explained why he was here. He was crazy. His gaze swept over her, focusing on her lips, still swollen from his kisses. The sight nearly caused him to become unglued all over again. He should get out of here fast, Rand warned himself.

But he didn't move and he didn't take his eyes off her. He had the most peculiar feeling of sinking into some kind of psychic quicksand, yet was unable, and unwilling, to try to free himself. No, he was definitely not in his right mind.

At that moment a weak meow sounded from the book deposit box. "Did you hear that?" Jamie murmured shakily. "Scotty said there was a kitten in there, and I came out to check."

Her voice trailed off, and she bent to unlock the box while Rand held the umbrella over them both.

There were four books, a letter, and a frightened, mewing kitten in the book drop. Jamie quickly scooped the creature up. She and Rand were still sharing the umbrella, so they huddled close together under it, their bodies touching. Once more pleasure shot through Jamie like sweet, golden flames.

Rand was unable to resist putting his arm around her waist. Strictly to keep her and the cat under the protection of the umbrella, he assured himself. But there was no way he could rationalize away the heat torching his body as he touched her.

"Another cat!" Jamie clutched the kitten and tried to ignore the beckoning warmth emanating from Rand's solid masculine frame.

His fingers tightened on her waist and began to knead with a light, slow pressure, so light and so slow, it was almost unnoticeable. But the effects of his touch were wildly discernible to Jamie. She felt a flow of molten liquid deep within, making her feel languid and weak.

Her nearness evoked a corresponding flame in Rand. He inhaled the clean fragrance of her hair and his body tightened. Two of his fingers slipped lower to the curve of her hip. She was a fascinating combination of curves and angles, both slender and softly rounded. He swallowed with difficulty.

"It seems to be all right," Jamie said, her voice husky. She cuddled the kitten while Rand continued to gently caress her.

"Poor little cat," said Rand, leaning closer. His breath rustled Jamie's hair. He brushed his lips against her temple and for one impetuous moment, she gave up the fight and allowed herself to fully relax against him.

They both sighed softly.

The rain fell harder, and the wind whipped cold droplets on them and the kitten, making it shiver. "We'd better get him inside." Jamie forced herself to move swiftly from Rand. But she couldn't stop herself from turning her head, to see if he was following her.

He was, and she began to tremble all over again.

"Let's take a good look at this little guy," Rand said, as they stood in the vestibule of the library. He reached over to pet the cat. It was coal black with yellow eyes and four white paws. "It looks like he's wearing high-topped sneakers," he observed dryly.

"That's a good name for him—Sneakers." Jamie caught her breath as Rand slipped his thumb beneath her hand to glide over her palm while his other four fingers continued to stroke the cat.

"That's too generic. And there's nothing generic about this kitten. He's a designer cat, no doubt about it. He needs a brand name...Reebok." Rand's thumb continued to make suggestive forays from her wrist to her palm.

She raised her eyes to his. The sexual tension hummed between them.

"Jamie, come home with me tonight," he said huskily.

Her heart seemed to lurch to a stop, then start again at breakneck speed. "No."

"You need to broaden your vocabulary." His lips curved into a wickedly beguiling smile. "You make too much use of the word no. Say yes, Jamie. You know you want to."

Had Eve and the serpent had a similar conversation concerning a certain piece of fruit? Jamie gulped. "I don't."

"You do," he said silkily. "And you will."

"Miss Saraceni, you got it! You got the kitten!" bellowed Scotty from across the library. He raced toward Jamie and Rand, followed by the other children.

Rand muttered a fierce curse. Jamie felt relief sweep through her. Things were moving too fast and she was too off balance to trust her judgment. She wasn't sure of her instincts any more, she wasn't sure of *anything* any more!

Except that she wanted Rand Marshall so badly that she ached with the force of it, and she didn't dare give in to her desires.

The children crowded around Rand and Jamie, all of them pushing and straining to reach the kitten.

"Can one of you kids take him home?" Jamie asked hopefully, and all the children expressed a desire to do so, then one by one disqualified themselves. Most of them lived in apartments that didn't allow pets; one child's brother had an allergy to cat hairs, three of the kids said an animal was too expensive to feed.

"You'll keep him, won't you, Miss Saraceni?" one of the children pleaded.

Jamie suppressed a grimace. She'd known all along it would come to this, but felt obliged to make at least a token protest. "With seven cats already at home—" she began.

Rand interrupted her, his tone incredulous. "Seven cats?"

She nodded. "And the only thing worse than living with seven cats is living with eight of them."

"That is a lot of cats," fifth-grader Ashley agreed. She turned to Rand. "Do you have any pets, mister?"

He shook his head, and the child beamed. "Then *you* can take the kitten home!"

"Me?" Rand was flummoxed.

"What a fantastic idea!" Jamie thrust the little black kitten into Rand's arms. "Here, hold him. Isn't he irresistible?"

"You're certainly managing to successfully resist him," Rand said dryly. A cat . . . and him? He'd never had a pet before; he'd even avoided the responsibility of plants. But the kitten was tiny and soft and mewed plaintively as it settled against him. Rand looked from the kitten to Jamie to the expectant faces of the children. The kitten's tiny pink tongue darted out to touch his hand.

"He's licking you!" cried Ashley. "He likes you! He knows you're his new dad."

"Mr. Marshall, we're all so grateful to you for giving our little library-box kitten a home," Jamie said, turning to Rand with a dazzling smile. Only he saw the gleam in her eyes.

"Laying it on a bit thick, aren't you?" he muttered. It was disconcerting to realize that he couldn't bring himself to refuse, not when Jamie was smiling at him in that certain way. He felt the sandpapery brush of the kitten's tiny tongue on his skin again. Glancing down at the newly christened Reebok, he faced the inevitable. He was well and truly stuck with this cat.

"Miss Saraceni, you said we could put up the St. Patrick's Day decorations today," piped up a skinny little girl with long blond braids.

"That's true, Tiffany," agreed Jamie. "They're in a folder on the big table in the activity room, along with some rolls of masking tape." Before she'd finished speaking, the kids were racing to the room at the back of the library.

Rand watched them go. "I'm trying to figure out how I got roped into this." He shook his head. "Never thought I'd see the day I'd be playing daddy to a cat!"

"It's a good way to get started," Jamie said dryly. "By the time you're daddy to a baby, you'll be a pro."

"A baby?" Rand laughed. "Me?"

"Why not? Don't you like children?"

"Sure. I like kids. And while I'm aware that single parenthood is in vogue, I firmly believe that a couple should marry before having a child."

"And, naturally, the smoothest of smooth operators has no plans for marriage."

"You bet I don't," he said breezily. "I like my life exactly the way it is. You, of course, want to get married," he added with a rather patronizing smile. "You've undoubtedly been dreaming of orange blossoms and white lace from the time you dressed your first Barbie doll in her wedding gown."

"My mother dressed the dolls. She's still dressing them. Mom's a doll dealer," Jamie explained. She was eager to drop the subject of marriage. Though she didn't know why, his irreverent attitude toward it depressed her. "Our house has thousands of dolls stashed in every room."

"*Our* house?" echoed Rand. "You live with your *mother*?"

His tone was similar to that of someone who'd been exposed to the bubonic plague and was asking about the symptoms. Jamie heard apprehension, disbelief and horror in his voice.

She was proud of her family and not at all apologetic about living with them. She told him a little about the seven Saracenis at home, not forgetting to include her older brother Steve, a frequent visitor, though no longer a permanent resident.

"All those people live in the same house with you?" Rand was aghast. "I haven't dated a woman who lived with her family since my teens, when all my dates were teenagers themselves."

"Then isn't it lucky that you're not dating me?" Jamie shot back.

"When I reached my thirties, I even gave up dating women with roommates," Rand continued wildly. No, he would not, he could not get mixed up with a woman whose living arrangements rivaled an episode of *The Waltons*. "You could invariably count on the roommate to appear at all the wrong moments." He grimaced at the memory. "What a major inconvenience!" But nothing like the presence of *seven* live-in family members!

"And you accused me of being a control freak!" Jamie said caustically. "A classic case of the pot calling the kettle black!"

"Exactly what do you mean by that?"

She smiled a superior little smile that set his teeth on edge. "I mean that you're as controlled, and controlling, as I am, if not more so. At least I live with other people who make it impossible for me to completely control everything in my life. You won't even risk that."

He stared at her, stunned. A lifetime of perceptions seemed to spin and shift like pieces in a kaleidoscope, and he saw himself not as a freewheeling, devil-may-care bon vivant, but as a rigid, regimented . . . control freak? He furiously sought to deny it, to her and to himself.

"You're way off base with your armchair analysis, honey. I happen to be the most spontaneous, live-for-the moment person I know. It's just that I hate inconvenience and demands and expectations."

His voice rose as he warmed to the subject. "I put up with all of that in my professional life, but not in my social life. The ideal Rand Marshall woman lives alone. She comes and goes as she pleases, just as I come and go as I please. There are no strings or ties, just freedom, independence and privacy."

Rand was positive that privacy and convenience would be unattainable with a woman who lived with *seven* members of her family. There would be curfews, schedules, obligatory boring chats with curious, expectant relatives. One thing was certain: hot sex and family life just didn't mix.

"I've never heard of a more sterile, lonely, unfulfilling life." Jamie was glaring at him now. "I feel sorry for you and your so-called ideal women. But then, maybe you deserve each other."

"Don't waste your sympathy on me," he said tightly. "And my life is *not* sterile or lonely or unfulfilling! Far from it!"

He thought of his house, his cars, his fat royalty checks. He'd achieved all of it on his own, independent of the Marshall family fortune and its strangulating restrictions. He could do what he wanted, when he wanted, wherever he wanted. There were no demands or expectations, not even on holidays, for his parents and brother had long been making their own holiday plans without including him.

"Well, don't let me stop you from returning to your terrific life," Jamie said, dismissing him with a chilly glance. "I have to check on the children now." She turned and walked away.

"Jamie," he called after her. He chose not to recall that only moments before, he'd been ready to relegate Jamie Saraceni to the far recesses of his memory because her living arrangements were inconvenient for him. Inexplicably, he couldn't seem to let her walk away.

"I'll need to buy some supplies and things for the kitten. I could use some advice on what and where to get it." He turned on the full force of the Rand Marshall charm, complete with engaging smile. "Will you come along? Living with seven cats qualifies you as an expert adviser. We'll go as soon as you're off work. Six o'clock, isn't it?"

"I'm sure you'll manage just fine on your own. The sales clerks in any pet store will be glad to help you," Jamie said, without looking at him.

She was hurt and angry—and determined to put Rand Marshall out of her thoughts for good. She'd watched him recoil as she'd talked about her family; he'd rejected her out of hand, and Jamie did not take rejection lightly.

She'd watched her handsome, charming brother reject woman after woman, time after time; she'd observed her sister's heartbreak when poor Cassie had been rejected by her womanizing, smooth-talking husband. All those years of witnessing rejection secondhand had bred a resolve in Jamie never to experience it personally. So far, she hadn't. She did the rejecting, by carefully screening whom she dated, by taking her leave the moment she sensed trouble in a new relationship.

She sensed big trouble now. Rand Marshall held a power over her that no other man ever had. The power to hurt her. Jamie's defenses roared into overdrive. She continued walking toward the activity room.

Rand's eyes filled with emotion. He was suddenly so consumed with fury, he wouldn't have been surprised if he ignited into flames. "If you walk through that door, you'll never see me again," he said in a low growl. "I won't play the role of besotted sap and besiege you with balloons and candy and flowers to raffle off."

She whirled around, her deep blue eyes as fiery as his. "Good!"

He stared at her, taken aback by her response. It wasn't the one he'd been expecting. "I'm not bluffing, Jamie," he felt obliged to point out.

"I realize that. You've already made it very clear that you won't waste your precious time on someone who's committed the unpardonable offense of living with her family."

He ran his hand through his hair in a gesture of frustration. She was besting him at every turn. A totally new experience for him. Women didn't argue with Rand Marshall, they pulled out all stops trying to please him. And he liked it that way!

What he should do—what any self-respecting Brick Lawson hero, oozing glib machismo would do—would be to get out now. He didn't have to put up with a stubborn, strong-willed control freak who refused to play the role he'd assigned her. He turned to leave.

Then it struck him. He wasn't going to talk to her again. He wouldn't see her smile, wouldn't kiss her. *Ever again.* He'd never get the chance to make love to her. Rand tried to identify the peculiar feeling that gripped him. Was it...loss?

Jamie pushed open the double doors leading to the activity room.

"Jamie."

The sound of his voice, deep and masculinely commanding, halted her in her tracks. She gazed at him, her dark blue eyes pensive and wary.

"When I heard you lived with your family, my first inclination was to head for the hills and not look back."

Jamie said nothing. Rand drew in a deep breath. "But I'm still here." His lips twisted into a self-mocking smile. "There are no hills to run to in South Jersey, the terrain is

relentlessly flat. And I still want you...to go out with me."
He took a step toward her. "Tonight?"

"I can't tonight, Rand." This was going to send him
screaming in the opposite direction. Though she knew it was
probably for the best, she ached inside. "The Merlton Elementary School is having its annual Spring Sing, and my
nephews are in it. So are all my after-school kids in there."
She indicated the group in the activity room. "I promised
I'd go."

It was beginning already, Rand thought, exasperation
sweeping through him with tidal-wave force. The intrusive,
never-ending demands of family interfering with his pleasure and convenience. This was no way to conduct a no-
strings affair!

Forget it, he said to himself. It won't work. The whole
idea was doomed from the start. "The Merlton Elementary
Spring Sing, eh?" He arched his brows. "You don't want to
miss that. And I wouldn't ask you to." Shrugging, he turned
to leave.

"Rand."

The sound of her voice stopped him cold.

"Would you like to come to the school program with
me?" Jamie asked impulsively. It was, she realized discon-
certedly, one of the very few times in her life that she'd acted
on impulse.

"Yes," he replied with such enthusiasm, it was as if she'd
invited him into her bed instead of to an elementary school
program.

He couldn't remember the last time he'd been elated over
the prospect of a simple date, but then, this was no ordinary date with a typical Rand Marshall woman. This was
Jamie Saraceni, and he was gleefully aware that she'd just
broken two of her cardinal dating rules—for him!

He hadn't had to undergo her telephone clearance, and
the separate-vehicle lunches had been preempted. He was
making progress with this woman who had so artfully
managed to madden and captivate him all at the same time.

A sudden shriek and the unmistakable sound of furniture being overturned in the activity room startled them both. The kitten meowed, reminding them of his presence and his needs. Reluctantly, Rand and Jamie parted to tend to their responsibilities, but not before Jamie gave Rand directions to her home in Merlton along with the time to arrive.

He left the library whistling a lively dance hit from a couple of years back. The lyrics extolled the excitement of knowing deep down inside he was breaking all the rules. He decided it was his theme song for tonight.

Five

It was still raining that evening when Rand parked in front of a small brick and frame house in a crowded residential section of Merlton.

Sometimes he stayed in the car and honked the horn to summon his date, particularly in inclement weather. Tonight Rand dutifully braved the torrent of blowing rain and walked to the front door.

Before he had time to press the bell, the door was flung open. He smiled at Jamie's undisguised eagerness. Oh, yes, she was thawing nicely, he congratulated himself. He wouldn't have long to wait. If tonight wasn't the night, she'd be in his bed by the weekend.

Except that it wasn't Jamie who'd opened the door with such flattering speed. It was her cousin Saran.

Rand suppressed the small—extremely small, he assured himself—twinge of disappointment rippling through him. He bestowed his most charming, designed-to-induce-a-swoon smile on Saran. "Hi, is Jamie ready?"

Saran didn't swoon. She gazed at him steadily. "I can't believe you're coming to this thing tonight," she said bluntly. "The Merlton Spring Sing is just awful. Even parents dread going to it. Don't you have anything better to do? Or are you *that* hung up on Jamie?"

Uncharacteristically, he had no ready answer to the questions. They were questions he didn't dare to ask himself. It was a relief when an old woman, dressed all in black, joined them in the tiny vestibule.

"Hello." She extended her small, blue-veined hand for him to shake. "I'm Mrs. Saraceni, Jamie's grandmother."

"Mine, too," interjected Saran. "So what if my dad was your nephew? You're still my grandmother to me."

"So what, indeed," the old woman agreed amiably. "Who are you, young man?"

Rand quickly removed his hands from his pockets, corrected his slouch to a military straight posture and shook her hand. "I'm Rand Marshall, Mrs. Saraceni. I'm pleased to meet you," he heard himself say in a tone and manner which would've pleased even his etiquette-obsessed parents.

The old woman's piercing black eyes seemed to pin him to the wall. She was very clearly assessing him and didn't care if he knew it.

"He's the guy from the library, Grandma," said Saran.

"Not the wacko dentist who sent the balloons and candy et cetera," Rand inserted swiftly, flashing a smile that had never failed to captivate and enthrall its female recipients.

Grandma shrugged. "Too bad. I wanted to meet that one. I particularly liked the milk chocolate butter creams he sent Jamie, and the candied almonds weren't bad, either. For a dentist, he sure pushed the candy. I'm half tempted to make an appointment at his office just to see him for myself."

Jamie chose that moment to appear in a pair of loose-fitting pleated tan slacks and an indigo sweater that accentuated the vivid blue of her eyes. The casual clothes enhanced her neat figure, her full, high breasts, small waist and softly flaring hips. Rand swallowed. The initial attraction he'd felt for her was nothing in comparison to the desire he felt for her now. He stared at her, his body beginning to throb.

"Hi, Rand," she murmured huskily. Her gaze swept his broad shoulders tapering to narrow hips and muscular thighs, and a reckless heat pulsed through her. He looked devastatingly sexy in his snug-fitting faded jeans and blue chambray shirt.

Her voice, her smile were infinitely alluring. Rand had to clear his throat before he could speak. "Hello, Jamie."

Their eyes clung beyond the time frame allotted for the exchange of simple, friendly smiles. Their gazes lingered and grew deeper, escalating swiftly to full-fledged awareness.

Both were oblivious to the watchful stares of Grandma and Saran. The old woman and the teenager exchanged glances of their own.

"Saran, get that box of Maureen's that we're supposed to drop off at the community center tonight," Grandma commanded in a voice that snapped Rand and Jamie out of their sensual daze.

"It's heavy, Grandma," whined Saran. "Can't *he* carry it?"

"Good idea." Grandma tapped Rand's arm. "The box is in the kitchen. Follow me, young man."

Bemused, Rand followed her into the kitchen, adjacent to the family room boasting two large television sets, sitting side by side. A big cat sat on top of each TV. Their tails were swinging in front of the screens like pendulums. Three more cats were draped over other pieces of furniture in the room.

A flash of black fur streaked by at the same moment that a Siamese cat, distinctly overfed, materialized from under the table. Standing on its hind paws, it dug its front claws into Rand's leg and let out a long, plaintive meow.

"Seven cats, hmm?" he murmured, striving for an enthusiastic note. He succeeded in sounding incredulous.

"Rand has a kitten," Jamie told the others with a grin while she shooed the Siamese away. "The two of them went shopping together this afternoon."

"Reebok rebelled against the shopping cart and nearly got us both evicted from the store." Rand couldn't tear his eyes away from Jamie's face. She had the most irresistibly appealing smile he'd ever seen. "Later tonight, you'll have to come over and check to see that I bought him the right stuff, Jamie," he added smoothly.

Before Jamie could reply, Grandma inserted herself into the conversation, pointing out the large brown box in the corner. Rand stared into it. It was filled with—"Dolls' heads?" he said aloud.

Dozens of vinyl heads, sporting hair of varying styles and colors, were piled on top of each other. Dozens of painted eyes and smiles seemed to leer up at him. "Uh, who decapitated them?" He tried to sound tactful. "And—why?"

"You would be amazed at what doll collectors will pay for some of these heads," said Grandma gleefully. "Maureen, my daughter-in-law, Jamie's mother, buys old dolls at yard sales, tosses out their broken bodies and cleans up and sells the heads at double and triple the prices."

"Oh." Rand stared down at the box of heads. "Interesting hobby, selling dolls' heads," he remarked politely.

"Maureen sells dolls, too," Grandma assured him. "She wants to start setting up for this Saturday's doll show and sale at the community center first thing in the morning. Would you mind delivering the box, Mr. Marshall?"

"We can stop on the way to the school," added Jamie. "Mom and Dad had to leave right after dinner with Cassie and the boys. I told Grandma and Saran that we wouldn't mind giving them a lift to the program."

"*We* wouldn't mind giving them a lift?" Rand repeated, catching Jamie's arm to detain her as her grandmother and cousin dashed to the car through the rain. "I don't recall you asking me how I felt about it."

She smiled up at him, her eyes bright. "Since I waived my telephone-and-lunch requirements for you, I didn't think you'd care."

It really wasn't funny, an indignant voice inside his head complained. He'd already declared himself the winner of this round, and now she'd turned the tables. But instead of fuming, he laughed. The joke was on him, and somehow he didn't mind. Not when Jamie was grinning at him, inviting him to share the humor, challenging him to try to best her again. He found himself looking forward to the evening ahead with a heated surge of anticipation.

"This car is, like, totally triumphant," Saran piped up from the small backseat of the Jag where she sat between Grandma and the box of heads. Her voice was filled with awe.

"One of those fancy foreign models," Grandma said tartly. "Must've cost thousands and thousands of dollars. And you're an insurance claims adjuster, Mr. Marshall?" Her tone went from tart to sardonic. "I never dreamed it was such a high-paying occupation."

It wasn't, of course. Rand felt color stain his neck and spread slowly to his face. Old Mrs. Saraceni was sharp.

"I hope you won't mind if I ask you a personal question, young man." From the old woman's tone, it was obvious that she would ask if he minded or not. "Are you on the take? Involved in something illegal to supplement your income? Because if you are, we'll just get out now and walk. We Saracenis don't associate with drug dealers or racketeers."

He could confess right now to being Brick Lawson of best-seller-list fame, of course, Rand thought. Maybe he should. After all, it was certainly preferable to being suspected of being a criminal! But he hesitated. Jamie was eyeing him warily now. He couldn't gauge her reaction to the revelation. What if she was furious that he'd been deceiving her and decided never to see him again? He wouldn't put it past her. She was stubborn and willful and completely capable of making her decision stick.

The prospect chilled him. He gave his head a slight shake. No, he couldn't risk it; the deception would have to continue. It was for a worthy cause, nearly a medical one: easing the raging fever that Jamie Saraceni had sparked within him.

As much as he disliked mentioning his background, it was safer than revealing his true career. Hadn't his family been affirming for years that his writing was not something to be proud of? They certainly never mentioned it if they could possibly avoid doing so. Rand automatically followed suit.

"You're right, Mrs. Saraceni, the salary of a claims adjuster would never cover this car." He paused. "I—have a trust fund and inherited family money."

"You come from a rich family?" Saran cried with unbridled enthusiasm. "That's so cool! My cousin Steve and I want to be rich. We want amazing cars that cost a fortune and Rolex watches and vacations all over the world." She leaned forward, her dark eyes bright. "Tell us about your life-style, Rand."

"A person has a life, not a life-style, Saran," Jamie said quietly.

"*You* have a life, Jamie, *I* have a life. If Rand is really rich, then *he* has a life-style," countered Saran knowledgeably. "Life-style depends on money. It's the clothes you wear and the crowd you run with and the car you drive. It's the food you eat and the house you own and everything that's inside it."

Jamie sensed Rand's discomfiture, but it was nothing compared to her own. Saran did have a point. There was a difference between a life and a life-style, between earning money and inheriting it, between living in Merlton and living in Haddonfield. All those differences, reaching into every area of life, heralded disparity and conflict to her. They were just more reasons she should keep a safe distance between herself and Rand Marshall, she lectured herself sternly.

"Look, there's a hitchhiker over on the corner on the left." Grandma's voice broke into Jamie's troubled reverie. "Holy saints, how could he risk his life that way? Do you know how many hitchhikers have been murdered over the years? How many have climbed into cars never to be seen again?"

When no one answered, Grandma launched into an astonishing recital of names, places and dates, garnered from her collection of monthly true crime magazines, dating back decades. "And then," she continued, "there's the flip side of the coin. The drivers who were murdered by the hitchhikers they picked up on the road." She proceeded to elaborate.

"There isn't one murder or disappearance that Grandma doesn't know all about," Saran said proudly. "She's read about them all."

"I see." Rand's lips twitched. The germ of an idea began to formulate in his mind. Suppose the intrepid salesman hero of his latest book had a grandmother with a predilection for reading about grisly crimes and making connections between them? Granny could simultaneously drive the hero, the villain and the police force crazy. After all, it was only fair that his characters should have to endure some of the frustration their creator was feeling these days, courtesy of the just-out-of-reach Jamie.

"And he was walking his dog and discovered the corpse." Grandma's sepulchral tones diverted him from his creative musing. "Incredible, the number of bodies accidentally found by people walking their dogs," she exclaimed with relish. "There they are, minding their own business, walking their dogs, when suddenly the dog bounds off into a wooded area or open field where the owner stumbles over a corpse."

Rand grimaced wryly. "That does add a whole new dimension to dog walking."

"I'm glad we have cats, Grandma," Saran said fervently.

Jamie sat quietly, not really listening. She'd grown up listening to Grandma's macabre facts; they'd long ago lost the power to alarm her. But she was alarmed by the questions, totally unrelated to homicide, that tumbled through her mind. Such as, who was Rand Marshall?

Admitting that the salary of an insurance adjuster wouldn't pay for his car was tantamount to admitting that he really wasn't working as one. So why had he told her that he was? He claimed to have a trust fund of inherited money, which implied a wealthy, privileged background. Was that a lie? Apprehension and anger surged through her. How could you trust someone who lied? When a man was dishonest about small things, a woman couldn't believe him when it came to more important issues.

Jamie didn't like this one bit. She withdrew behind a protective facade of silence.

Saran had been right on target about the show, Rand thought glumly as he shifted uncomfortably in the backbreaking metal chair in the Merlton Elementary School gym. The Spring Sing was truly terrible. The gym was packed, hot and humid; the children couldn't carry a tune, although the loudspeakers broadcast their discordant little voices at earsplitting volume. If there was a hell, this was it, he decided, and contemplated being trapped here at the Spring Sing for all eternity.

Worst of all, Jamie sat beside him, not speaking to him or even glancing in his direction. She'd been aloof and withdrawn during the drive over, and now she seemed to be deliberately ignoring him.

He felt ill-used and sulked a bit, but noted that Jamie didn't seem to notice, or care. Though she was sitting close enough to him in the overcrowded gym that their shoulders brushed, he sensed that she was far away from him.

"Isn't that Ashley? The kid from the library, standing on the right in the third row?" he whispered, leaning closer, his lips almost touching her ear. He inhaled the elusive, enticing fragrance she wore, and it went straight to his head like a shot of one-hundred-proof bourbon. He wanted her attention so badly, he would do anything to get it, even feign interest in this abysmal show.

Politeness required Jamie to turn her head toward him to nod. Their faces were close; if each moved forward just a few inches, their mouths would be touching. She stiffened and quickly pulled back, determined not to respond to a liar, no matter how sexy and attractive he happened to be.

Rand felt a stab of desire so strong it was almost painful. His eyes focused on her mouth, memorizing its seductive shape, remembering its sweet taste and passionate response to his kisses.

"Point out your nephews to me," he murmured, shifting in his chair so that his thigh pressed against hers. The more cool and aloof she became, the more determined he became to get close to her, to win a softly intimate smile, to see her eyes dilate and darken with arousal. Just for him.

Jamie ignored his request the first three times he made it. The fourth time, when he raised his voice above a whisper, she decided she'd better point out Brandon and Timmy, just to shut him up.

But Rand couldn't seem to spot them in the mob of children. He had to lean closer, to put his arm around her shoulders to better position himself to follow her line of vision. His other hand found her hand and lifted it, ostensibly to admire her blue star sapphire ring. But after studying the ring, he didn't relinquish her hand, he laced his fingers with hers.

Against her will, a shiver of response streaked through her. She felt surrounded by him. His leg was pressed tightly against the length of hers, his arm was around her, holding her subtly but inexorably against the strength of his big male frame. His thumb began to stroke her palm in that arousing caress that had so unraveled her in the library earlier to-day.

Jamie let out a shaky breath. All her feminine instincts urged her to close her eyes and relax. But she didn't dare. She had too many doubts about Rand Marshall to simply let herself go.

More than once Jamie had been told that she had a will of iron. Sometimes it was said with amusement, sometimes with admiration, often with exasperation. But it took every ounce of her famed iron will to make herself move firmly out of Rand's hold. After she had, she sat tense and stiff on the edge of her chair, her back straight and unyielding.

Her rigid posture should have been off-putting; she'd certainly intended it to be. But before Rand could take offense at her snub, she tilted her head slightly and her shiny black hair fell forward, revealing the nape of her neck.

Rand forgot that she'd just brushed him off like a pesky gnat. He couldn't take his eyes from her nape. It was sexy, soft and vulnerable, and he knew that she would be very sensitive there. The urge to touch that elegant, silken curve was overwhelming. He felt something hot flicker inside himself.

Leaning forward in his chair, he cupped her nape with his hand and lightly caressed her with his fingers.

Jamie's heart slammed against her ribs, and she quivered like an arrow in a crossbow. Her surroundings seemed to fade into the background, and she was suddenly impervious to the heat of the overcrowded gym, to the jostling, noisy audience and the children's cacophony. All her senses were focused on Rand's touch.

Slowly, his fingers began to trace a light, sensual path down her back, following the fine, straight line of her spine. She felt him pause at the line of her brassiere concealed under her sweater, then carefully smooth over its outline. From his light exploration he would learn that there was no clasp there and could deduce that it was front-fastening. The thought of him acquiring such intimate information about her sent a tremor through her.

When his hand reached the small of her back, he began a slow, gentle massage. Hot ribbons of fire laced her belly. She had to swallow the moan of pleasure rising in her throat.

"Don't!" she whispered hoarsely.

"Why not?" His husky rasp, both soothing and seductive, made Jamie's mind cloud. "I like touching you and you like me to touch you." His fingers slipped beneath the hem of her sweater and touched her warm, bare skin.

Jamie shot out of her chair with the speed of one escaping fire. She felt as if she really was burning from the hot flames Rand's touch ignited in her. She walked swiftly from the gym to a side corridor leading to an exit. It was cool and dimly lit in the deserted hallway. Pulses racing and knees shaking, she leaned against the tiled wall, trying to regain her equilibrium.

It was a lost cause. Rand had followed her and was striding along the corridor toward her. Jamie's eyes widened. He was carrying the raincoat and umbrella she'd left behind in the gym.

"Our minds are running along the same track," he said with a definitely unholy gleam in his light brown eyes. "The sooner we get out of here, the sooner we can be alone."

Her heart seemed to do a funny somersault. "I came out here to get away from you, not to be alone with you," she said, flushing.

He stared pointedly at the emptiness of the corridor. The two of them were completely alone; even the racket from the gym was muted.

"I don't think I want to believe you." He smiled a slow, sexy smile of anticipation as he dropped her coat and umbrella to the floor and moved to stand directly in front of her. "I think you're as hungry for this as I am."

Curving his hands around her upper arms, he slowly, inexorably drew her to him. His movements were unhur-

ried, his grasp loose, giving her every opportunity to object, to break away from him if she were so inclined.

But she wasn't. She couldn't. The newly awakened passion he'd inspired within her conquered her self-imposed
course of rectitude. Jamie gazed into his mesmerizing eyes
and didn't move, breathe or utter a word of protest.

Rand slid his hands to her shoulders and massaged them
lightly. He used his solid strength to pin her against the wall
and fit his body to hers. Jamie felt the cool tile against her
back while the masculine heat of his frame warmed her in
front. She felt boneless and languid, and a dizzying sense of
inevitability swept through her. He was going to kiss her,
and she was aching to feel his mouth on hers again.

Her legs felt too rubbery to support her. Reflexively, her
fingers grasped the front of his shirt and she held on tight.
While their eyes held, he lowered his head and touched his
mouth to hers.

For a second or two, he moved his lips lightly against hers,
coaxing them to part. And then, as if he could wait no
longer, he angled his head to seal their mouths together.

Jamie whimpered as passion flowered within her once
more. Her arms slid around his neck and she nestled her
body against him, trying to get even closer. She welcomed
the velvet penetration of his tongue as it thrust hotly into her
mouth. Uttering a soft moan, she kissed him back, gliding
her tongue over his, tasting him, drawing him in more
deeply.

Rand groaned with pleasure and gripped her tightly, sliding his hands along her slender curves. When he finally tore
his mouth from hers, he pressed it against the sensitive arch
of her throat.

"I want you so much, Jamie. Let me have you. Come
home with me tonight." He closed his eyes as a fierce spasm
of need spun through him. "I can't wait any longer, baby.
You're driving me out of my mind."

The force of his impassioned words brought her back to
her senses. "No, Rand." Jamie was alarmed. Not only

couldn't she trust him, she couldn't trust herself, either! She knew that her willpower increased in direct proportion to her distance from his arms. Swiftly, she slipped from his embrace to stand several feet away from him.

"Jamie, you know you want me." He knew he sounded a bit desperate, but he didn't care. He was desperate. "Sweetheart, it'll be so good between us. I'll make you feel things you've never felt before."

"And then what, Rand?" Her blue eyes flashed fire. "After we've gone to bed and you've made me feel things I've never felt before, what then?"

Rand stared down at her, his expression bemused. He'd always prided himself on his quick wit and facility with words. He was a right-brained person, one of his ex-girlfriends who'd read all about such things had once told him. But the clever right side of his brain seemed to be temporarily immobilized. At this moment, all he was capable of doing was to gaze at Jamie with passion-glazed eyes and echo: "What then?"

"You haven't thought beyond getting me into bed," Jamie exclaimed, angry with him and even more angry with herself for succumbing so completely to his kisses.

"That's a loaded question." Rand's right brain was functioning enough to realize that.

"It's not a question, it's a statement of fact. You want to go to bed with me."

"From the moment I laid eyes on you," Rand confessed huskily.

She thrilled to his admission and at the same time seethed with anger at his shallow, short-term expectations. Never had she felt so ambivalent. "You're sexually attracted to me, but you're not in love with me," she accused. Yet the romantic within her yearned for him to swear that he'd fallen in love with her at first sight while the realist inside proclaimed he'd be lying if he did.

"How could I be in love with you?" He gave his head an exasperated shake. "For God's sake, Jamie, we hardly know each other!"

Uh-oh! Rand grimaced. If he were a character in a cartoon strip, a light bulb would be drawn over his head. He laughed slightly, without mirth. "The very point you were trying to make, of course. But you led me into making it myself."

Jamie took her raincoat from him and shrugged into it without saying a word. Rand watched her. Her fingers trembled a little as she fastened the belt. She looked small and vulnerable and incredibly desirable. Unable to stop himself, he reached out to stroke her cheek with the palm of his hand.

"Is it so important to you that your lovers be in love with you before they take you to bed?"

He felt a peculiar sting at the thought of Jamie falling madly in love with other men and subsequently permitting them to make love to her. The sting increased to a full-fledged pang at the image of her lying naked and aroused in bed, opening her arms to one of those nameless, faceless males in her past. He felt shaken, confused. Until now, sexual jealousy had been unknown to him.

"Obviously, being in love with your lovers and having them in love with you isn't one of your top priorities." It took effort to keep her voice cool, but Jamie succeeded.

"You're making this far more complicated than it is, Jamie," he complained. "It's really very simple, very basic. We want each other and we're both consenting adults. True, after meeting your grandmother, I can understand your reluctance to skip off blithely with a stranger. She's compiled a body count that's downright chilling. But surely you know by now that I'm hardly the type to abduct you and rape you."

"And leave my corpse in a wooded area to be stumbled over by some poor innocent dog and its owner on their daily walk?" Jamie put in, her eyes agleam.

Rand tried and failed to suppress a swift grin. "We're getting as macabre as your grandmother. Do you think it could be catching?" Remembering the topic at hand he frowned, his eyes narrowing with determination. "Don't change the subject, Jamie. We were talking about you and me and why we should—"

"I can see that seduction is serious business to you with no time out to joke or kid around," Jamie interrupted again. "Well, here's my answer to your offer for quick, emotion-free, involvement-free sex. No, thank you."

"It wouldn't be quick." He gave a sharklike smile. "Believe me, honey, I've never had any complaints in that department."

Without another word, she walked away from him.

"Jamie, come back here," Rand called after her, his voice rising in frustration. "You can't expect me to keep chasing after you."

"I don't." She slowed her pace and turned around. "I expect you to move on to your next successful conquest. That's exactly what Steve would do. Because when everything always comes easily, you resent having to put special time or effort into anything that doesn't. So you don't bother, you only take what's easy."

That struck a nerve. Rand did the only thing he could do when feeling defensive. He seized the offense. "One of the things I hate most is being compared to the other men in a woman's past. Another is having to hear pat analyses of my character." And then, because he couldn't stand it, he asked. "Who's Steve?"

"My brother. You'd know that if you'd bothered to listen to me, but you haven't because you're not interested in learning anything about me or my life and the people in it. All you want from me is sex."

"Not again!" Rand groaned. "We've already had this conversation, Jamie. We're going in circles."

"That's because nothing's changed and nothing is going to change. I don't want to be rushed and you want to rush me into bed. We're at a hopeless impasse."

"And you don't want to be rushed," Rand muttered. "What do you want? A *courtship* or something?"

"You said courtship with the same repugnance that a temperance league member must've used to say liquor," Jamie said dryly, unable to suppress a smile. "But I happen to like the idea of a nice, old-fashioned courtship, and I'm going to hold out for one. Not with you," she added quickly. She took a deep, steadying breath. Though it hurt, she was determined to face reality. "We'd never work out. We're on two totally different wavelengths."

"To say the least," Rand agreed quickly, too quickly.

Jamie fought back the pain of his speedy dismissal. It was for the best, she insisted to herself as she resumed walking.

To stop her, Rand knew that he'd have to promise more than he felt like giving. And he didn't want to; he didn't have the time or the inclination. A courtship? Dammit, he wouldn't do it. Why would he want to court—what a foppish word!—a demanding, stubborn woman with hopelessly outdated values and a will of iron? Jamie Saraceni would cheerfully and unapologetically turn his life upside down—it was at half-tilt already, thanks to her.

Rand frowned. He liked his life—life-style, according to the mercenary little Saran—exactly the way it was. Or the way it had been before he'd made his first fateful trip to the Merlton Library.

He jammed his hands deep into his pockets and watched Jamie reenter the gym. For a few moments, he stood in the empty corridor, then strode purposefully to the main entrance of the school.

Six

He was standing near the door a half hour later when the program ended and the crowds began to emerge. Grandma and Saran spotted him before Jamie did. At least, they acknowledged him first.

"Hello there, Rand," Grandma called loudly as the three worked their way through the crowd.

He waved to her, noting that somewhere between the beginning and end of the program the Saraceni matriarch had relegated him to first-name status. But if he was making progress with the grandmother, it was all downhill with her granddaughter. Jamie didn't even glance in his direction.

"Before we leave, we'll have to tell Maureen and Al that Jamie, Saran and I are going to your house to check on your kitten," Grandma announced.

"I see them, Grandma. I'll tell them and be right back," called Saran. She blazed her way through the crowd with the finesse of a bulldozer.

Old Mrs. Saraceni had included herself and Saran in the invitation he had issued exclusively to Jamie, noted Rand. He should've been aghast. Instead, he felt relieved. He knew that Jamie had no intention of going to his house; now her grandmother had taken the decision out of her hands. For the first time ever, he viewed a woman's family members as something other than an annoying hindrance.

Grandma continued to elbow her way through the throng of people, finally giving Jamie a shove that propelled her to land directly in front of Rand. He reflexively put his hands on her waist to steady her.

He didn't want to remove them, even when it became obvious that she didn't need steadying. He wanted to touch her, to keep her close. He'd spent the last half hour fighting an internal civil war about whether to stay or leave. Though he was still here, he didn't know if he'd won or lost the war.

"Rand's changed his mind, Grandma," Jamie said, removing herself from his grip while carefully averting her eyes from his. "He doesn't want us to go with him. Come on, we'll catch a ride home with Mom and Dad."

"There's no need to refer to me in the third person," Rand inserted archly. "I'm perfectly capable of speaking for myself. I do want you to go with me. I'm quite concerned about the cat. I want to make sure everything I bought for him is right."

"Right," Grandma repeated dryly. She looked from Rand to Jamie, rolled her eyes and shook her head.

Rand's sleek stucco and tile house was a radical departure from the brick colonials and wooden gingerbread-style houses that comprised most of the architecture in Haddonfield. It was located at the end of a cul-de-sac on two acres of ground landscaped with tall pines, shrubs and an assortment of flowering bushes not yet in bloom.

He pulled the car into the long circular driveway and pressed the button of his automatic garage door opener. The heavy door glided open and he drove the Jaguar inside, parking it next to a midnight-blue Ferrari Testarossa.

"You have two of the most excellent cars I've ever seen!" exclaimed Saran. "I can't wait to tell Steve about them."

"Steve," Rand repeated. "Your cousin. Jamie's brother." He cast a triumphant glance at Jamie, who hadn't spoken to him during the entire drive to Haddonfield.

"You see, I do listen to you, Jamie," Rand added righteously, in case she'd missed the significance of his observation.

Jamie had no comment. She deliberately remained silent as Rand led them through a passage from the garage to the house. But her first sight of Rand's living room rendered her truly incapable of speech. She'd never seen a room quite like this one. It was the size of a gymnasium, all black and white, chrome and Lucite. A huge metal sculpture—at least she assumed it was supposed to be a sculpture and not a bicycle wreck—was hung on one stark white wall.

There were no lamps. Track lighting illuminated certain areas of the room. Her eyes flicked from the floor-to-ceiling windows that comprised one wall to the black leather upholstery on the low-slung furniture, if the collection of backless, armless and legless circles, squares and rectangles could be called furniture.

"Is the whole house like this?" Jamie managed at last. Grandma and Saran were still staring around the enormous room, looking as awestruck as Dorothy on her arrival in Oz.

Rand nodded. "I think Debbie—she was the decorator—called it minimalism. I told her I wanted something different, and she came up with this."

"Different doesn't quite describe it," drawled Jamie. Debbie. She pictured a platinum blonde, size 38-D, poured into a leopard print jumpsuit made of spandex; a bombshell who slithered over the leather banquettes when she wasn't slithering all over Rand.

"Minimalism," Grandma muttered. "I guess I can see where that came from. Minimal color, minimal comfort, minimal taste—at maximum prices, of course."

"Yeah." Saran grinned. "This place looks like a video of a bad dream."

Reebok, drawn by the sound of voices, chose that moment to make his entrance. His tiny paws skidded on the smooth black tile floor, and he slid into one of the thick white shag rugs. He arched his back and hissed ferociously at the rug, then attacked it on a leap.

"Even the cat's black and white," observed Grandma. "Lucky for him, he fits right in with the color scheme."

Rand shrugged, grinning. "I can see you're all underwhelmed with the decor. I can't say I like it much either, but I've gotten used to it."

"How long have you lived here, Rand?" asked Saran.

"A year." Though ostensibly he was answering Saran, his attention was fixed on Jamie. She was staring at the black and white ceramic logs in the black faux marble fireplace. "I had an apartment in New York for years and finally got tired of the pace and the hassles of living in a city that size."

"Ah, a midlife crisis victim, though yours hit earlier than most," Grandma said knowledgeably. "I've watched plenty of them tell their stories on TV. You needed a complete change. Next thing, you'll wake up sick of being single." She cast a shrewd black-eyed gaze on Jamie. "You'll want to get married."

"And hire a new decorator," added Saran.

Rand shifted uneasily. He still had trouble understanding his feelings of discontent with the city life he'd once thrived on. But he certainly didn't care for Grandma Saraceni's diagnosis. "I positively refuse to classify a simple desire for life in a smaller, less hectic town as a midlife anything! I've never gone in for conventional angst, and I'm not about to start now. Some friends in the Philadelphia area recommended Haddonfield to me. I saw it, liked it and moved here."

He was getting bored with the conversation. Never had he felt less like talking about himself. He felt restless and on edge; he wanted action, excitement. He wanted sex. His light brown eyes focused longingly on Jamie's lovely profile. Since action, excitement and sex were out, he would settle for a private conversation with her. As one who seldom chose to compromise, Rand deliberately avoided examining his sudden talent for it.

"Everything I bought for the kitten is in the kitchen. Would you look over it, Mrs. Saraceni?" he asked, lacing his tone with respectful deference. "Jamie, may I have a word with you? Privately?"

"Of course, of course," said Grandma benevolently. "Saran, bring that cat into the kitchen with me."

The moment they left the room, Jamie turned to Rand. "What's the point?" she asked wearily.

"I want you to define courtship," Rand cut in swiftly. "Dinner dates? Movies? Miniature golf games? Good-night kisses on the doorstep with the porch light shining in our faces? Those sorts of things?"

"If you're trying to make it seem juvenile and ridiculous—"

"I've succeeded?"

"You really are a rich man," Jamie said suddenly, distracting him with her seeming non sequitur. "When you said you were earlier, I wondered if you were lying. Now I'm sure you're not. The cars, this house, are proof of that. So I have to ask what kind of game you're playing, Rand Marshall."

"Game?" he repeated, stalling for time. Did he dare risk telling her about his Brick Lawson pseudonym and success?

"You're not an insurance claims adjuster." Her eyes flashed. "You lied about that. And I can't help but wonder what else you've lied about. Why did you come to the Merlton Library, Rand? This time I want the truth."

"Did growing up among your grandmother's police gazettes account for your suspicious, investigative bent of

mind?'' he asked lightly. There was a certain irony in being
highly paid as a master storyteller but bungling the tale he'd
spun for Jamie, he decided wryly. If only he'd had an editor on hand to point out the gaping holes in his plot.

Now the question was: How much could he tell her without permanently alienating her? "You're right, I don't work
for an insurance company," he began carefully. "I only said
I did because I needed a plausible explanation for being in
Merlton. The real reason I came to the library was to see
you." He kept his eyes fixed on her face, gauging her reaction.

If the tense set of her jaw, her clenched fingers and snapping blue eyes were correct indicators, her reaction to his
partial confession wasn't favorable.

"Why did you want to see me? You don't even know
me." She glared at him, anger coursing through her. "I want
you to be honest with me, Rand Marshall. Do you have a
sister who made the unfortunate mistake of falling in love
with my brother Steve? Did you come seeking revenge because Steve dumped her? Did you decide that the way to get
back at Steve was to make *his* sister fall for you and then
break her heart?''

"Are you crazy? Of course not!" Rand gaped at her incredulously. "I don't even have a sister. Your revenge
scheme is a plot straight out of daytime television, Jamie.
People don't do things like that in real life."

"Oh, yes, they do," Jamie said grimly.

His eyes widened. "You mean it's actually happened to
you? The irate brother of one of your brother's rejectees
attempted some romance revenge? Using you?" It sickened
him to think of Jamie being used, being hurt. No wonder
she was so cautious, so mistrustful....

Jamie nodded her head. "Believe it or not, it's happened
twice, two years apart. Eric Crenshaw and Richard Aldero.
Oh, I'll never forget those wolves in sheep's clothing. Both
were brothers of women who were foolish enough to think
that Steve would eventually make a commitment to them.

Of course, he broke up with them when they tried to get serious. Their brothers believed in the old 'eye for an eye, tooth for a tooth, dumped sister for a dumped sister' philosophy and came to romance and reject me as vengeance against Steve."

"Did they succeed?" Rand asked quietly.

"No." Jamie shook her head. A flash of disillusionment shadowed her eyes. "I found out what was going on before I could be hurt. Steve wasn't even surprised it happened. He said he'd do the same for me, and if I ever got dumped I should let him know."

"I know hell hath no fury like a woman scorned and all that, but somehow I can't see you unleashing your Don Juan brother on a mission of vengeance against some guy's unsuspecting sister."

"I'd have to get dumped first, wouldn't I?" Jamie said coolly. "And that's not going to happen." She gazed at him steadily. "I didn't meet you till you came into the Merlton Library. How did you know about me?"

Rand took a deep breath. "I know Daniel Wilcox, Jamie. And he hasn't exactly been reticent about wanting to go out with you. When I heard you'd unequivocally turned him down, I became curious about you."

"So you came to Merlton to check out the woman who wouldn't date your dentist?"

"I know it sounds ridiculous, Jamie."

"It certainly does. Too ridiculous to be true."

"Jamie, it's the truth! I found it hilarious that Wilcox couldn't get a date with a librarian, so I came to Merlton expecting to have a good laugh. Then I saw you." His voice deepened roughly. "And the laugh was on me. I took one look at you and felt as if I'd been kicked in the gut, I wanted you so much."

Was she losing her grip on reality or did his story actually have a ring of truth to it? Jamie wondered. She wanted to believe him, so much it scared her. On full alert now, the tough practical side of her nature abruptly suppressed the hopeful romantic within her.

"Well, a rich man like you might get a temporary kick out of consorting with the working class, but I'm under no illusions that it would be anything but short-lived."

"So now it's a class conflict between us," growled Rand.

"We're all wrong for each other," Jamie said firmly. The facts were all there; if only she could convince herself to believe them!

"So you keep saying." Rand's tawny gold eyes gleamed with masculine challenge. "Fast hot sex versus true love. Blue blood versus blue collar." He took a step toward her. "Can you come up with anything else?"

"Isn't that enough?" A sudden wave of danger coupled with a churning excitement streaked through her. She tried to still her racing pulse by sheer force of will. It didn't work. "I want to go home now, Rand. I'll call my grandmother and Saran."

"Not just yet." Rand closed the gap between them.

Jamie gasped softly at the contact of his warm, hard body. His hands moved slowly, tantalizingly down the length of her back to her hips, melding every inch of her intimately against him.

"I don't think our differences are all that insurmountable," he drawled softly, nuzzling the sensitive curve of her neck. "Not when we want each other so much."

Jamie caught her breath as he curved his fingers deeply into her rounded bottom at the same moment his teeth closed lightly around the lobe of her ear. Flames of fiery excitement licked her abdomen. "I won't go to bed with you," she insisted with a breathless, soft moan.

"I know. Not until I've courted you." Rand smiled against her lips, then nibbled sensuously at them. "And so I've decided to give this courtship thing a shot. I'm beginning now, with the good-night kiss. Minus the doorstep and the glaring porch light."

His mouth closed over hers, hot and forceful, and Jamie arched against him, quivering with wild pleasure at his touch. She seemed to become more sensitized each time he kissed her, her response coming faster and hotter, her control slipping faster and farther away.

She locked her arms around his neck and kissed him back, her passion escalating to match and meet his own. When he finally tore his mouth from hers, it was to string a chain of hungry, stinging kisses along the length of her throat, pausing at the rapidly beating pulse in the tender hollow.

He groaned. "We're dynamite together. Are you sure you don't want to skip the miniature golf games and all the rest and head straight for the bedroom?"

Jamie chuckled unsteadily. "I'm sure." She rubbed her nose against his in a spontaneous gesture of affection. She was elated. Finally, there were no more lies standing between them. He'd been honest with her, and he'd just agreed that he was willing to work toward a relationship based on respect, friendship and trust, instead of aiming for a quick fling based solely on sex.

She felt closer to him, as if the passionate emotional fire of their kiss had melted away the barriers that stood between them. It was a relief to stop fighting him, an even bigger relief to end the battle with herself. Jamie put aside her caution and ambivalence. She was going to see Rand Marshall, to date him, to get to know him.

And then... Jamie stared up at him with dreamy eyes. Did she dare allow herself to believe that their future held the possibility of what she'd always dreamed of? A deep, mutual love to last a lifetime?

She has bedroom eyes, thought Rand as desire slashed through him. He imagined her gazing up at him with those big, gorgeous blue eyes of hers as she lay in his bed, hungry and open for him. A courtship, ridiculous and old-fashioned as it might be, was definitely worth his time and energy if it meant realizing his goal: to make love to Jamie Saraceni.

His dreams of the future included the arousing, provocative scene of the two of them entwined in ecstasy on his king-size water bed in his black and white bedroom.

It was unusual for the American Public Library Association's annual conference to generate any news, but this year an account of its opening meeting made page two in the Philadelphia newspaper, and Jamie read it intently. As the Merlton Library's limited budget did not include a single dime for traveling funds, she'd been unable to attend the Dallas conference. But she was keenly interested in the proceedings, for this year's agenda was to include the problem of libraries being used as day-care centers.

Her eyes flicked to her own group of library latchkey kids, who were scattered around the library, the younger ones playing in the toy corner, the older ones seated at tables doing homework or reading books. It had been difficult to get them settled down today; they'd all been infected with Friday afternoon, living-for-the-weekend fever. Jamie had a mild case of it herself.

She turned back to the article. Some libraries in the big cities, where hundreds of children might seek refuge daily, had restricted access by allowing no children into the library unless accompanied by an adult. Others had gone even farther and warned that leaving unsupervised children could result in abandonment charges.

The measures seemed unduly punitive to Jamie, but she could understand the concern to protect library liability. Since she'd begun her unofficial program, the number of children spending after-school hours here had doubled. Fortunately, Merlton was a small town, and the numbers were still manageable. But suppose they increased to crisis proportions? Jamie reread the article, looking for an answer. Unfortunately, it only reported the facts and offered no solutions.

She was so lost in thought that she jumped back with a gasp when a hardcover book was slammed down on the desk in front of her. She jerked her head up, and her blue eyes connected with Rand Marshall's teasing brown ones. "You startled me," she said breathlessly.

"You nearly jumped out of your skin," Rand corrected. "What were you daydreaming about?" His grin widened. "Or perhaps it's *who*?"

"I was wondering what are the alternatives to turning librarians into baby-sitters." Her blue eyes sparkled. She was thrilled to see him. Since he'd left her at her door last night most of her thoughts, excluding the ones centering on her young patrons, had been of him.

"Wrong answer, honey. When a man asks you who you're daydreaming about, you're supposed to say his name. Here. It's all in the book." Rand handed her the book he'd banged down on the desk. "I found it in the bookstore this morning. Maybe you need it more than I do."

The book's title, *Guide to a Modern, Old-Fashioned Courtship*, made Jamie smile. She gazed brightly up at Rand. "Have you read it?"

"I read chapter one. It suggested giving memorable little gifts in the beginning of the courtship, something whimsical like helium-filled Mylar balloons or something traditional, like flowers or candy. But remembering what happened to the luckless Daniel's tokens of esteem, I decided against that route. I'm donating my traditional and whimsical items directly to their eventual recipients. So here's a box of milk chocolate butter creams for your grandmother." He laid a beautifully designed pound box of candy on the desk. "And—"

He stepped into the vestibule and returned a moment later with two dozen colorful Mylar balloons on long strings. "Here, kids," he called out. "They're all yours." The children descended upon him, grabbing for the balloons. "Okay, gang," he said heartily. "Let's see you work off some of that end-of-the-week energy. Take your balloons outside and run around the library a few times."

"It's chilly—" Jamie began.

"It's fifty degrees and sunny," countered Rand, but he called to the children. "Wear your coats, kids. Uncle Rand doesn't want anybody to catch cold." He lowered his voice to add for Jamie's ears only, "But he sure does want to get rid of the little tykes to steal a few minutes alone with the librarian."

Jamie flushed a delicate pink. The kids charged boisterously out the door, balloons bobbing in the air.

"*Uncle* Rand?" she echoed, making a valiant attempt to sound nonchalant. His virile, compelling masculine presence made her feel uncharacteristically giddy and highstrung.

"The book says that if your courtship partner likes children and animals, it's a good idea to show how well you get along with the little critters. Yesterday I impressed you with my devotion to kittens, namely Reebok. Today, I'm trying to wow you with my natural, genial way with kids. Are you wowed?"

She smiled. "Oh, definitely, Uncle Rand."

"Great. Now can we skip ahead to chapter five? That's when we allow ourselves to get carried away by our mutual passion and proceed directly to the bedroom."

Jamie laughed; she couldn't help herself. The man was outrageous and incorrigible. And he was very hard to resist. "Sorry, but I never skip chapters. I never read the ending of a book until the very end, either."

"That figures." He shrugged. "Well, since you won't go to bed with me yet, come with me to the Blarney Stone tomorrow. It's *the* place to be on St. Patrick's Day, even if you're not Irish. They have Irish songs and authentic corned beef and cabbage, not to mention green beer, Irish whiskey and Irish coffee."

"I'd love to go. But be sure to wear green tomorrow, or Mom won't let you into the house," Jamie warned playfully. "She's full-blooded Irish. Her maiden name was O'Reilly, and she takes St. Patrick's Day very seriously."

Look what we've got for you:

5 FREE GIFTS

... A FREE 20k gold electroplate chain
... plus a sampler set of 4 terrific Silhouette Desire® novels, specially selected by our editors.

FREE MYSTERY GIFT

... PLUS a surprise mystery gift that will delight you.

All this just for trying our Reader Service!

If you wish to continue in the Reader Service, you'll get 6 new Silhouette Desire® novels every month—before they're available in stores. That's SNEAK PREVIEWS for just $2.24* per book—26¢ less than the cover price—and FREE home delivery besides!

Plus There's More!

With your monthly book shipments, you'll also get our newsletter, packed with news of your favorite authors and upcoming books—FREE! And as a valued reader, we'll be sending you additional free gifts from time to time—as a token of our appreciation for being a home subscriber.

THERE IS NO CATCH. You're not required to buy a single book, ever. You may cancel Reader Service privileges anytime, if you want. All you have to do is write "cancel" on your statement or simply return your shipment of books to us at our cost. The free gifts are yours anyway. It's a super-sweet deal if ever there was one. Try us and see!

Get 4 FREE full-length Silhouette Desire® novels.

Plus this lovely 20k gold electroplate chain

Plus a surprise free gift

▼ PLUS LOTS MORE! MAIL THIS CARD TODAY ▼

Silhouette's Best-Ever "Get Acquainted" Offer

Yes, I'll try Silhouette books under the terms outlined on the opposite page. Send me 4 free Silhouette Desire® novels, a free electroplated gold chain and a free mystery gift.

225 CIS JAZA (U-S-D-03/90)

PLACE STICKER FOR 6 FREE GIFTS HERE

NAME _____

ADDRESS _____ APT. _____

CITY _____

STATE _____ ZIP CODE _____

Offer limited to one per household and not valid to current Silhouette Desire Subscribers. All orders subject to approval. Terms and prices subject to change without notice. © 1989 HARLEQUIN ENTERPRISES LTD.

PRINTED IN U.S.A.

Don't forget...

... Return this card today and receive 4 free books, free electroplated gold chain and free mystery gift.

... You will receive books before they're available in stores.

... No obligation to buy. You can cancel at any time by writing "cancel" on your statement or returning a shipment to us at our cost.

If offer card is missing, write to: Silhouette Books®
901 Fuhrmann Blvd., P.O. Box 1867, Buffalo, N.Y. 14269-1867

BUSINESS REPLY CARD
First Class   Permit No. 717   Buffalo, NY

Postage will be paid by addressee

Silhouette® Books
901 Fuhrmann Blvd.
P.O. Box 1867
Buffalo, NY 14240-9952

No Postage
Necessary
If Mailed
In The
United States

He'd managed to put out of his mind the obligatory rite of politely interacting with her family when he picked her up for their date. Rand suppressed a sigh. The rules of courtship weren't easy at all. But keeping his end goal in mind, he merely smiled and said lightly, "So you're half Irish and half Italian. An interesting combination. Italian passion and Irish fire."

"I've always considered myself a practical, dependable, in-control American."

Rand's eyes gleamed. "I like my imagery better." He checked his watch. "I have a few errands to run before I pick you up tonight. I'll be here at six."

"Tonight?" She stared at him. "We—we don't have a date tonight."

"We do now." He leaned forward and kissed her forehead lightly before heading to the door. "See you at six," he called jauntily.

Jamie gulped. "Rand, I can't go out with you tonight." That stopped him dead in his tracks. She swallowed again, harder. "I already have plans."

His smile faded, and the warmth abruptly drained from his eyes, leaving them a glittering shade of gold. "We played this scene last night, Jamie. I was a good sport and accommodated myself to your plans. Now it's your turn to do the same for me."

"But I can't—"

"If you have a date, break it," he growled. "I won't tolerate you seeing other men." The words slipped out, words that cool, casual Rand Marshall had never felt the need to say. The fact that he'd said them now stunned him, alarmed him, too. But he didn't retract them.

"I don't have a date, not with a man," Jamie said quickly. "Some of my friends and I—"

"Girlfriends?" At her nod Rand smiled, the tension draining from him. "Oh, well, if you're just going out with the girls, it's no big deal. Call them and tell them you have a date. Girls understand that men come first in their friends' lives."

Jamie's jaw tightened. "I don't know what kind of women you've been spending time with, but I happen to value my friends. We made these plans weeks ago, and I can't back out. It's one of my oldest and closest friend's birthday, and three of us are taking her out to dinner."

"If it's her birthday, I guess you can't back out," Rand conceded with a long-suffering sigh. He didn't bother to mention the time that a woman he'd been dating for just two weeks had passed up attending her brother's wedding to take a weekend jaunt to the Bahamas with him. Jamie not only wouldn't approve, she'd likely take offense.

"I want you to understand that I'm not pleased, Jamie. This is the first time in my life that a woman has chosen to spend an evening with her girlfriends over an evening with me."

"Then too many women have spoiled you," Jamie said archly. "You can't expect everybody to rearrange their schedules to suit yours."

"Do you know who you sounded like just now?" Rand frowned fiercely. "Didactic, prim and righteous Martha Elizabeth Healy, the scourge of my elementary school years. She was *the* insufferable girl, every class in every school has one, whom the teachers always picked to sit at their desks when they left the room to write down the names of the students who misbehaved."

"Hmm, let me guess. You always misbehaved, and Martha Elizabeth always wrote down your name. And to add insult to injury, you couldn't charm her into erasing it." Jamie laughed.

Much to Rand's consternation, Jamie was right. Now, as a free-thinking, free-living adult, he was about to willingly embark on a courtship of a Martha Elizabeth clone?

He felt trapped, thwarted and wildly frustrated. By the time he'd driven to his house, he'd also talked himself into feeling insulted. When Daniel Wilcox phoned an hour later to offer him a blind date, a model, just Rand's type, Rand decided that he had every right and every reason to go.

Seven

Jamie and her friends, Angela Kelso, Romaine Abramovic and Charlene Spencer, claimed a table for four at Darby's and opened the oversize menus sporting watercolor illustrations and calligraphy script. The place was crowded, noisy and smoky with the Friday night revelers in full swing. Jamie tried not to wish she weren't here. After all, it was Angela's twenty-fifth birthday, a milestone of sorts, and Jamie and Romaine and Charlene had agreed to treat her to the meal of her choice at the restaurant of her choice. After dinner, Angela had insisted upon coming here, and in keeping with the spirit of birthday indulgence, they'd all complied.

"I think I'll have the amaretto ice cream float," Angela said, laying down her menu to gaze searchingly through the crowd lining the bar, which was elevated on a platform and surrounded by a thick brass rail. "It's too delicious to pass up. And it *is* my birthday," she added, a trifle defensively.

Jamie's eyes connected with Romaine's, but neither spoke a word. It was Charlene who said frankly, "You can't really want a big ice cream drink after that huge meal we just had, Ange. Why not have diet soda instead?"

"Why don't you come right out and say it, Charlene?" Angela cried, flushing. "You think I'm fat!"

Jamie winced. Over the years, she'd watched Angela go from a slightly plump child to a chubby adolescent to finally evolve into a young woman, at least thirty pounds overweight, who was alternately depressed and defiant about it. Jamie and Romaine judiciously shied away from mentioning Angela's weight problem. Charlene didn't.

Fortunately, the waitress arrived to take their orders and the subject was dropped. Jamie and Charlene ordered diet sodas, Romaine a glass of white wine and Angela, rather defiantly, the amaretto ice cream float.

"You're not going to believe who just walked in," Romaine said, lowering her voice, though the band was so loud she could have shouted and still not have been overheard. "The Cherry Hill heartthrob himself, Daniel E. Wilcox, D.D.S."

"He's here? Are you sure?" Angela turned scarlet and dug into her purse to nervously remove her compact, lipstick and comb.

"You knew he was going to come here tonight, didn't you, Angie?" guessed Charlene. "That's why you were so insistent that we stop here."

"I know he often comes here on weekends." Angela was primping frantically. "I—I thought there was a chance that he might be here. Oh, God, how does my hair look? Is my eyeliner smeared?"

"You look fine, Ange," Romaine said soothingly.

Jamie suppressed a groan. Not Daniel Wilcox! The weeks of his unwanted pursuit had strained her relationship with Angela, and Jamie regretted the awkwardness that had sprung up between them because of it. She'd hoped that it would swiftly dissolve when Wilcox stopped pestering her.

Now they were all here together, and she couldn't guess what was going to happen next.

Charlene was facing the crowd and gave a report to the others at the table. "Brace yourself, Angela. Your dream boat dentist is here with someone. A blonde. Tall, gorgeous. Great clothes. She looks like a model."

Angela seemed to crumple in her seat. Her three friends exchanged dismayed glances. "Some birthday present. Poor Angela," Romaine whispered to Jamie, who nodded glumly.

Rand followed Daniel and the two willowy blondes, his date and Daniel's, to a booth in the corner of the restaurant. After placing their orders, the women excused themselves to go to "the little girls' room."

Rand cringed at the euphemism. His date irritated him immensely, although he conceded that it wasn't really her fault. He acknowledged that she was sexy, attractive and desirable; furthermore, she'd made it plain that she was available and quite willing to further their acquaintance. There was a time when he would have been eager to take her up on what she was offering.

But not now. Tonight, he was restless, bored and distracted. He was not being charming or attentive to his beauteous blind date. His thoughts were all of Jamie Saraceni, who had not only infiltrated his mind, but seemed to have taken it over completely. He could hardly wait for this evening to end; he wanted to drop off his date and call Jamie, no matter how late the hour. He wanted it to be tomorrow night when he would see Jamie again and take her into his arms and— "Hey, there's Angela Kelso! She's the dental hygienist at my office." Daniel's voice roused Rand from his reverie. "I should go over there and say hello. It's her birthday today, and I forgot to mention it to her." He frowned, his eyes mirroring regret. "I meant to get her a card, but then Shelli called."

Daniel stood, then gave a low whistle. "Damn! Jamie Saraceni is here, too. She's sitting at the table with Angela."

Rand bolted from his seat. "Where?"

Daniel pointed out the four young women at the table across the room. "Jamie's the black-haired one, sitting next to Angela, who's the one with the light brown hair."

Rand squinted. Though he certainly knew Jamie, he played dumb. "There are two girls with light brown hair at that table."

"Angela is the one that's, uh, slightly overweight. She's really a great girl," Daniel added quickly. "She's my right arm at the office. Rand, come over to the table with me. I want to say hello to Angela but I'm not thrilled with the prospect of facing Jamie Saraceni. Not after the way she, uh, uh . . ."

"Ground your ego into the dust?" Rand suggested dryly.

Daniel scowled. "I bet you can't get any farther with her than I did. In fact, I dare you to try."

Rand shrugged uncomfortably. As much as he wanted to see Jamie, he did *not* want it to be under these circumstances. He was here with a date, and he wasn't eager to have Jamie find that out. Those odd feelings he'd been having all evening, of being disloyal to Jamie, of being *unfaithful* to her, returned in full measure, and he couldn't seem to banish them. "Look, I'll just stay here at the table and wait for Shelli and Maxi to come back."

"They won't be back for a long time. Look at that line!" Daniel gave Rand a friendly shove. "C'mon, Marshall. Are you afraid to face the fact that Jamie Saraceni won't give you the time of day, either?"

Rand grinned. He couldn't help himself. "Oh, she'll give me the time of day, all right." Remembering her impassioned responses to his kisses, his smile broadened. She'd already given him a lot more!

"I'd like to see you prove that." There was a conspiratorial glint in Daniel's eyes. "I'll even sweeten the incentive. A weekend this summer at my time-share condo in Cape May if you get a date with her.''

"Are you crazy? A bet? This is real life, not some dumb TV sitcom, Wilcox.''

"I'll raise the stakes even higher. If you get her into bed, you can have the condo over the Fourth of July weekend, the biggest weekend at the shore. Hey, I think they've spotted us. Let's go.'' Daniel propelled Rand through the throng on the small makeshift dance floor, around the bar, to the table where Jamie and her friends were sitting.

"He's coming this way, Angie!" Charlene said excitedly. "Now act cool. Don't melt into a puddle at his feet.''

Jamie's chair was facing the wall, rendering her unable to witness Daniel Wilcox's advance firsthand. But Charlene reported that the dentist was not alone; he was being accompanied by a male friend with "to-die-for" good looks.

Was there a patron saint of dating? Jamie wondered nervously. If so, please let Daniel Wilcox be nice to Angela and not slaver all over me, she silently implored.

"Happy birthday, Angela!" Daniel's jovial tones echoed around the table. "I bet you thought I forgot! Wrong! I have a card to give you on Monday.''

"Oh, thank you, Daniel,'' Angela said in breathless euphoric tones.

"Why don't you introduce my friend Rand Marshall to your friends here,'' Daniel continued, grinning slyly.

Jamie whirled around in her chair to meet the deep golden eyes of Rand Marshall. For a moment, she was too astonished to speak, and by the time she recovered, Angela had already made the introductions.

"Do I get a dance with the birthday girl?" Daniel asked Angela in that slick, unctuous way of his. But Angela blushed with pleasure and quickly stood up. "Rand, why don't you ask Jamie to dance?" Daniel continued in those same cloying tones.

Rand looked at Jamie and raised his brows. Jamie rose from her chair and allowed him to lead her onto the small, crowded dance floor.

"Look at the expression on Wilcox's face." Rand laughed softly as he drew her into his arms to dance. "He thinks we just met, and he can't understand why you'd consent to dance with me when you wouldn't even give him your phone number."

"Look at the expression on Angela's face," Jamie said soberly, watching the other couple slow dance. "She looks positively enraptured. If only she'd realize what an undeserving creep Daniel Wilcox really is."

"Daniel's not that bad." Rand proprietarily placed her arms around his neck, then clasped his own hands tightly around her waist. She felt small and soft against him. Her arms were locked around his neck, her body pressed tightly to his, her legs slightly apart to accommodate the fullness of his swiftly hardening masculinity. A deep shudder of need shook him. "I never expected to run into you here tonight, Jamie."

She felt his response and her heart began to thud as a liquid heat throbbed inside her. "I didn't expect to run into you, either," she murmured huskily. But, oh, she was glad that she had!

"We're still on for tomorrow night, aren't we?" He brushed his lips against the silken texture of her hair. One big hand slipped lower to hold her intimately against him.

"Are we?" Jamie's voice shook. The sensations he was evoking within her were so intense they were dizzying. "I wasn't sure, after the way you stomped out of the library earlier this afternoon." She smiled, suddenly able to see the humor in it, though she'd been upset at the time by his abrupt departure. "You accused me of being like that nasty Martha Elizabeth creature who plagued your school days. I was never the class commandant, Rand, honest." She drew back a little and smiled at him.

"I can believe that." He grinned. "You were probably the prom queen."

She laughed at that. "Me? Not hardly. I was just a quiet girl who studied hard and spent most of my spare time at my job. I was a paid library aide in Cherry Hill from the time I was fifteen."

"And that's when you decided to become a librarian," he concluded.

Jamie nodded. "I love reading and books and I love every moment I spend in the library." She paused and her eyes sparkled. "Well, almost every moment. There have been a certain few I could do without."

"Just as there are a certain few books you could do without," Rand said carefully, testing the waters. "All of Brick Lawson's, for example."

Jamie laughed. "How true! To quote a literary sage: That isn't writing, it's typing!"

The metaphorical waters were definitely too chilly to risk exposure, Rand decided. He'd just begun to nibble on her neck when the music abruptly ended. The band announced that they were taking a break, and couples moved slowly from the packed dance floor.

Rand made no motion to leave, and Jamie stared at him expectantly. Those eyes of hers were so expressive, he could almost read her thoughts. She was waiting for him to suggest joining her and her friends; driving her home later would naturally follow. If only he'd come to Darby's without a date! Unfortunately, he hadn't.

He cleared his throat. "I'd like to offer you a ride home tonight," he began.

"Thank you," Jamie replied at once. "My friend Romaine drove tonight so she can take Charlene and Angela home."

"You didn't let me finish, honey. I said I'd like to offer you a ride home tonight. But I can't."

"Oh." Jamie studied the tiled floor.

"I'm here with a date," Rand finished baldly.

Her eyes flew to his face, and her cheeks turned crimson. With humiliation for setting herself up for the fall she'd just taken, courtesy of Rand Marshall's announcement. And with sheer, unadulterated rage. She was jealous! Jamie realized with horror and pure fury. Never had she felt such wild, searing anger. For the first time in her life she felt possessive of a man, and the throes of sexual jealousy were the result. She hated it; she hated him.

"Fine," she said tautly, walking away from him. "Then go back to your date."

Rand sighed and reached out to catch her hand, jerking her back to him. "Here we go again. How many times are you going to stalk off in a snit and how many times am I going to have to drag you back and calm you down?"

"Don't bother! Just let go of my hand and—"

"I asked you out for tonight, Jamie, but you turned me down. And I don't recall the two of us signing any exclusionist contract."

Her first reaction was defensive. "For your information, I don't have snits!" Followed by a counteroffensive. "And I think you have a lot of gall to dance with me like *that* when you're here with another woman!"

"I wish I weren't here with another woman. I wanted to be with you tonight, Jamie. It's your choice that I'm not."

What could she say now? Jamie wondered vexedly. It was true. Furthermore, he was absolutely right. They hadn't even tacitly mentioned limiting their company exclusively to each other. She pulled her hand free. There was no argument she could present, much as she wanted to. "I want to rejoin my friends now. And I'm sure your date is waiting for you."

Although she'd broken their physical contact, his glittering eyes held her captive. "Do you want me to dump my date here and now? I could arrange for Daniel to take both women home. Then you could be with me."

Jamie fought back a dizzying surge of triumph. She felt a primitive sense of victory in having him claim her, over and in spite of, another woman. This had certainly never happened to her before, especially since Jamie avoided triangles as firmly as she avoided rakes, rogues and superficial charm boys.

But her well-ordered mind quickly took charge of the reckless elation bubbling through her. She was not in competition with Rand's date, and he was not a trophy to be won, she reminded herself. And she knew herself well enough to realize that her momentary glee would inevitably give way to guilt.

"Don't dump your date," she said, sighing resignedly. "It wouldn't be fair to her. My brother Steve does things like that, and I've never approved."

"And you won't bend your principles, even to suit your own purposes," Rand concluded thoughtfully. "That's . . . admirable."

"I can do without your sarcasm," Jamie snapped. "You've made it very clear that you think rules are made to be broken!"

"I wasn't being sarcastic. And there's a difference between rules, values and principles." He gave a world-weary, self-mocking smile. "Not that I adhere to any, of course."

She stared at him. He didn't sound as if he were bragging. His tone wasn't flippant and his eyes... She gazed into their depths. She couldn't identify what she saw there, but she did know it wasn't bravado or self-satisfaction.

Daniel Wilcox chose that moment to join them, having already escorted Angela to her table. "C'mon, Marsh. We'd better get back to Shelli and Maxi," he said purposefully, glancing from Rand to Jamie with narrowed eyes. "They're aspiring models down from New York, auditioning for a lingerie ad to be shot in Philadelphia," he added, directing this comment to Jamie with a smug smile.

"I'm impressed," she said flatly. Privately, she congratulated herself on having the good taste to have never considered, even for a moment, a date with Daniel Wilcox.

"I'll see you tomorrow night, Jamie," Rand said, and his voice was firm, daring her to challenge him.

She didn't. "Good night, Rand," she said coolly and walked to the table where Romaine, Charlene and Angela were eagerly awaiting her.

"Tomorrow? You have a date with her tomorrow?" Daniel croaked and launched into an impassioned soliloquy. "That means you've won a weekend at my condo this summer! How did you do it? What did you say to her? How come she'll go out with you and not me? Damn, I never thought... What if you get her into bed? I have *plans* for the Fourth of July weekend, Rand! It's my annual saturnalia!" he ended on a half-wail.

Rand glanced at him, thoroughly astonished by the distaste and disapproval flowing through him. This was the first time he'd ever viewed Daniel's superficial approach to life and to women as anything different from his own. He didn't understand it, but he realized that either he was changing or Daniel was.

And when Rand went home alone that night, leaving Daniel with two amorous, inebriated, sexy young women, Rand had to face the fact that it wasn't Daniel who'd undergone any kind of transformation. It was himself.

March weather was always unpredictable, and the temperature on St. Patrick's Day shot up to an amazing, unseasonable seventy-five degrees. Rand put aside the green sweater he'd planned to wear to the Blarney Stone and settled for a dark green knit polo shirt. It was still warm and a balmy breeze was blowing lightly when he arrived at the Saraceni's door promptly at eight o'clock.

"Come in, come in!" Grandma Saraceni greeted him warmly, taking his arm and pulling him inside. She was wearing a black dress, but had pinned a green plastic shamrock to its bodice in tribute to the Irish saint. Saran, wearing a blindingly bright lime-green T-shirt and shorts, stood behind the old woman.

"No flowers or candy?" Saran surveyed him with disapproval. "Nothing at all?"

"Saran, run upstairs and tell Jamie her young man is here," Grandma instructed firmly. "And tell her to hurry up."

Saran shrugged and sauntered off.

"You come with me and I'll introduce you to Jamie's mother and father while you're waiting for Jamie." The old woman took Rand's arm and pulled him along after her, introducing him to Maureen, a pretty woman with delicate features, dark hair and deep blue eyes like Jamie's.

"Cassie, Brandon and Timmy aren't here. They went out for a pizza and a movie. But you can meet them next time," Maureen told him with a bright, friendly smile. She was dressed all in green and was sitting at the kitchen table, taking cash from a cigar box and arranging the bills in piles, the coins in paper rolls. A big, black cat leaped onto the table and tried to fit himself into the cigar box. Maureen laughed and kept on counting.

"Money from the doll show," Grandma Saraceni said, following the direction of Rand's gaze. "Remember those dolls' heads you dropped off at the community center? Maureen sold every one. Along with some dolls, too, of course."

Next he was introduced to Jamie's dad, Al Saraceni, whom Grandma proudly described as "my son, the master carpenter."

"Rand, you look like a fellow who likes a glass of wine now and then," Al said expansively. A commercial jingle extolling the virtues of a certain brand of soap blasted from the TV. The Siamese cat was sprawled on top of the set, sleeping soundly.

"You don't mix drinking with driving, do you?" Grandma interjected quickly, her dark eyes piercing.

Rand glanced from one to the other, uncertain how to answer either of them. Were these trick questions, leading into some sort of trap?

While Grandma quoted accident statistics involving alcohol, Al presented him with a bottle of wine. It had a handwritten label pasted on it.

"For you. Saraceni Sour Cherry Wine." Al beamed. "Wine making is one of my hobbies. I grow the fruit in my garden and have a wine press set up downstairs in the basement. Take it home and enjoy it."

"Drink it when you're at home and plan on staying there," Grandma added darkly. "We don't need any more maniacs out there on the highways."

A loud, sharp blast of a car horn sounded above the traffic noises from the nearby highway. "It's Todd. See you later!" called Saran from the front of the house.

"Midnight, Saran," Al shouted back.

"Uncle Al! The party won't break up till at least two o'clock!" howled Saran. "You don't want me to be the first one to leave."

"We'll leave the porch light on and wait up for you, dear," sang out Maureen. "See you at midnight."

Saran gave a shriek of disgust and slammed out of the house.

Rand contrasted the room-to-room shouting to the hushed, modulated tones in the Marshall household. Despite the fierceness of the "conflict of opinions"—Marshalls never quarreled, of course—voices or hands were never raised. Disapproval, Marshall-style, was expressed by cold, relentless silence. He was certain that wasn't the case here.

Rand shifted uneasily. "What happens if Saran's late?" he asked hesitantly. Al was a strong, tough-looking man. Would the young woman need the protection of Child and Youth Services if she disobeyed her uncle?

"Oh, Saran's never late." Al chuckled. "She knows her curfew and keeps it, but she carries on that way every time she leaves the house. She likes to sound off."

"Saran is very intense. She has a flair for drama," Maureen put in. "Unlike Jamie. Jamie has been calm, cool and collected since the day she was born." Her voice held a wistful note of regret.

Rand thought of the times when Jamie had definitely lost her cool with him. He could definitely describe her as intense, and she'd never been remotely calm or controlled in his arms. So all that was out of character for her? He smiled, pleased with the insight.

"Jamie has a good head on her shoulders," Grandma announced. "Saran should follow her lead. Jamie never dated punks who honked their horns for her. She only keeps company with quality gentlemen." She nodded toward Rand. "You think Saran could land a man like him? Think again."

Jamie arrived just in time to hear her grandmother's frank pronouncement. She smiled weakly. "I'm ready to leave, Rand."

Rand's eyes slid over her. She was wearing a kelly green silk dress with wide, short sleeves. A thick belt accentuated the smallness of her waist, and a full skirt came to the top of her knees. Her high-heeled strappy green sandals made her legs look long and shapely. Suddenly, Rand couldn't wait to get her out of there and have her to himself.

They made their goodbyes and left the house. "Whew!" Rand heaved an exaggerated sigh of relief as they strolled down the front walk. "I half-expected your dad to order me to have you in by midnight."

Jamie smiled. "There are no such rules for me. I've had my own key for years. In fact—" she paused, her cheeks flushing a little "—my folks would probably be thrilled if I were to roll in at six or seven in the morning. They'd think I was finally, um, loosening up. I'm afraid they see old maid written all over me."

"But not Grandma. She likes you just the way you are." He opened the car door for her and settled her inside, acting the role of perfect gentleman. Then he grinned. Grandma Saraceni was watching from the window, making no effort to conceal her presence. He waved to her and she waved back.

"You definitely have a fan," Jamie said dryly as Rand slipped behind the wheel. She'd been watching the window byplay between Rand and her grandmother. "Well, I suppose it's only natural. Grandma dotes on Steve, and you're a lot like him."

"Hmm. Steve. The Lothario who loves 'em and leaves 'em so ruthlessly that he's inspired a brotherly hit squad to seek romantic revenge through you. Thanks a lot, Jamie. Next you'll be telling me I'm a Daniel Wilcox type."

"Aren't you?"

"No!" Instead of starting the engine, Rand turned to Jamie, his expression serious and intent. It was very important to him that she recognize the differences between him and the Daniel Wilcoxes and the Steve Saracenis of the world.

"You see, I—" He paused, frowning. What *were* the differences? It baffled and annoyed him that he couldn't pinpoint them on demand. Vaguely, he realized that it was his feelings for Jamie that now separated him from the pack he'd blithely belonged to for years. But how could he put that into words without revealing too much?

"If I were like them, you wouldn't be here with me," he said at last.

"I guess that's true," Jamie said with a nervous laugh. "Unless I've suffered a massive lapse in judgment and am making the biggest mistake of my life."

"You aren't making a mistake being with me." Rand studied her as a wave of hunger washed through him. His body was throbbing with needs that, according to the rules of courtship, weren't going to be met tonight.

Frustration rippled through him. To hell with courtship; he would give seduction another shot. "I haven't told you how beautiful you look tonight, Jamie." His voice lowered. "And how much I want to be alone with you. Let's forget the Blarney Stone and go to my place."

She stared at him impassively.

"Your father gave me a bottle of his homemade wine," Rand persisted. "We can open it and toast St. Patrick in the comfort and privacy of—"

"I only drink my father's wine when I have a bad cold. It not only opens the sinuses, it knocks you out more successfully than that nighttime liquid cold medicine. Dad's sour cherry wine is about six-hundred proof."

"Whoa! Then we'll definitely go directly to my place." He laughed softly, intimately. "I'll even make your parents' day and bring you home late tomorrow morning."

She didn't blink an eye. "Do you want to hear my answer or can you guess it on your own?"

He took her hand in his and lifted it to his mouth, brushing his lips across her palm. "I know what you'd like to answer. Yes. I've felt your response to me, the way you melt in my arms, the way you go up in flames when I kiss you. Let's make tonight the night."

Gently but firmly, she withdrew her hand. "Is this the routine pitch you make at the beginning of every date? And do women actually buy it?"

He wasn't about to tell her how well that particular spiel had worked for him. She'd either accuse him of lying or laugh. Determined to gain any advantage, he pressed on. "Don't try to play it cool, Jamie. I know it's all an act to mask how much you want me. Your parents say that you never lose your head, but I can make it spin, baby, and we both know it. You want to go to bed with me."

"If we're taking my family's observations as truths, then according to Grandma, I've landed you. Is that true, Rand?" Her smile mocked him. "Shall I ask Daddy to send a deposit to the Sons of Italy hall for our wedding reception?"

They sat, silently challenging each other. Rand fought a desire to pull her into his arms and kiss her senseless, but somehow he felt it might backfire on him, rendering him senseless as well.

Jamie battled an equally strong urge to lean toward him, wrap her arms around his neck and pull his head down to her. She didn't dare. She'd lost control once too often in his arms to fully trust herself to stop.

As if by mutual consent, both leaned back in their seats, as far away from each other as they could get in the confines of the sleek, low-slung Ferrari.

"Wedding reception?" Rand gave a hoarse, forced laugh. "Don't hold your breath, honey."

"Me? In bed with you?" She smiled sweetly. "Don't hold your breath. Honey," she added with a cool laugh.

"You'll be in my bed long before we star in any wedding reception at the Sons of Italy hall," promised Rand.

Jamie said nothing at all.

Her silence unnerved him. She was so controlled, so self-possessed. Paradoxically, he admired her for holding her own with him as much as he wanted her to surrender to him. "Before we leave for the Blarney Stone, *not* my place, I have something for you. Here." He thrust a small box at her. It was wrapped in bright green tissue.

She flashed a grin. "One of those whimsical or traditional tokens recommended in chapter one in the courtship book?"

"I jumped ahead to chapter two. It calls for mementoes of certain, specific shared experiences and events."

"We haven't shared any experiences or events," she reminded him. "Unless it's a memento of the Merlton Spring Sing?"

"Believe me, that's one event I don't want to commemorate. Now will you open the box?"

"You really shouldn't have, Rand," she said, self-consciously unwrapping the package.

"According to your cousin Saran I most definitely *should* have. I could see her brand me as a cheapskate with no style when I showed up at the door without flowers or candy. No doubt she had black orchids and imported Swiss chocolates in mind."

"Probably." Jamie laughed. "Saran leads a rich fantasy life." She removed the paper and opened the box. A small gold shamrock on a thin gold chain gleamed in its nest of green velvet. "Oh, Rand, it's beautiful!" she exclaimed. "I've never seen one like it."

Rand shrugged. Though he wouldn't admit it, her thrilled response gave him a warm glow of pleasure. He'd never been one for impulsive gift giving. But the impulse had struck today, and his joking references to *Guide to a Modern, Old-Fashioned Courtship* had nothing to do with it. Not that he'd tell her that!

"I thought St. Patrick's Day was specific enough to qualify under the chapter two guidelines," he said gruffly, shrugging again.

Jamie leaned across the seat and gave him a swift spontaneous hug. "It's wonderful, Rand. Thank you so much." She lifted it from the box. "I want to wear it. Will you fasten it around my neck?"

He did, taking his reward by stroking the soft, creamy skin at her nape. He had to close his eyes, so great was the force of desire that gripped him. He was unable to keep himself from kissing her. Her arms went around him, and she kissed him back. It was a long, hot kiss that left them both breathless.

When Rand finally started the car and pulled away from the curb, he had Jamie's hand tucked under his, resting on his thigh.

From a downstairs window in the Saraceni house, Grandma let the curtain fall back into place and moved away, humming an off-key medley of "That's Amore" followed by Mendelssohn's "Wedding March."

Eight

The Blarney Stone in Philadelphia was a quiet Irish restaurant and pub all year long, except on March seventeenth, when it served green beer and provided live music to hordes of revelers, at least three quarters of whom had not a drop of Irish blood in their veins. By the time Jamie and Rand arrived, a line had formed to get inside and was already snaking down the block. Rand ignored it, taking Jamie's arm and escorting her directly to the front door. He murmured a few words to the bouncer on duty, shook hands with the enormous hulk of a man, then the two were admitted.

"What did you say to him?" Jamie asked. "I heard someone say that everyone in the line had reservations."

Rand grinned. "Why bother with reservations when greasing his palm with a few bills is so much more dependable?"

"You bribed that man to let us in?" Jamie frowned. "I don't think I approve, Rand. All those people who were here ahead of us, waiting in that long line. It just doesn't seem fair.''

"I like to look on it as spreading the wealth. And both sides mutually benefit." Rand took her arm. "Come on, I see a table for two. Let's grab it."

Jamie remained where she was, suspicion taking root within her. She fixed him with a stare. "That's how you persuaded Saran to give you my phone number, isn't it? You bribed her!''

"I wanted the number and Saran wanted the cash." Rand's smile was teasing. He put his arm around her waist and pulled her close. "Why are you getting so upset? Because I haven't made use of the number and called you?''

"That's not the issue here and you know it!" Jamie said coldly, removing his hand from her waist and stepping away from him. "I don't like my impressionable young cousin learning to—to accept payoffs!''

The ice-blue coldness of her eyes and the fierceness in her tone immediately put him on the defensive. "Jamie, there's nothing wrong with paying for certain favors or privileges. It's the way of the world, the way things are done."

"You mean that's the way things are done by slick, spoiled rich boys who think they can buy their way through life."

Rand didn't like the sound of that. He'd been fighting against the elitist upper-class label for years. "Tipping generously hardly falls into—''

"Tipping generously?" Jamie interrupted. "You do have a way with words. You've managed to change bribery into tipping generously with the sleight of your tongue. I suppose you were generously tipping Saran when she gave you my phone number?''

He stiffened. "Do you always have to have the last word?''

"Only when I'm right."

"A moot point. As far as you're concerned, there's never a time when you're not right!''

She wished she had a ready, scathing comeback. Unfortunately, none came to mind. Rather than sputter irately, she forced herself to remain silent, folded her arms tightly in front of her chest and surveyed the laughing, singing, dancing crowd, all in various shades of green, hoping for inspiration to strike. It didn't, but she did see a familiar face. An extremely handsome one, which had made female hearts beat faster since his kindergarten days. Her brother Steve.

A flash of amusement rippled through her. She should have guessed that Steve Saraceni would be here tonight. If the Blarney Stone was the place to be seen on St. Patrick's Day, then of course, Steve would appear. As a dedicated trendsetter and trend follower, he was always in the right place at the right time.

Steve spotted her at the same time she saw him. His handsome face broke into a wide smile, and he immediately pushed his way through the crowd to reach her.

"Hey, babe, what are you doing here?" he asked, lifting her off her feet and swinging her around in the air.

Rand watched the display, fighting the sickening tide of emotions crashing through him. The guy with the movie-star looks was hugging Jamie with a familiarity claimed only by longtime friends or lovers. And Rand could tell at a glance that the guy wasn't the type to have women as friends. And the way Jamie was looking at him....

Rand swallowed. He'd seen her glance at good-looking Daniel Wilcox as if he were a bug to be squashed. But the humor and affection in her big blue eyes as she gazed at the muscular hunk who hadn't yet set her back on her feet conveyed a wholly different message.

Oh, yes, she had a past with this man. With all her caution, reserve and suspicion about "smooth operators," he should have guessed that she'd been badly burned by one. And this guy, dressed expensively in green right down to his high-topped sneakers, moved with arrogant grace and supreme confidence, and looked like a winning contender for the premier smooth operator title.

"Take a walk on the wild side. Dance with me." Steve took Jamie's hand and pulled her along with him to the dance floor. A dance team, direct from the Emerald Isle, was instructing the wild, giddy crowd on how to perform an Irish jig.

Jamie glanced at Rand. He was staring at them, his expression grim. She dug her heels in and refused to budge another step. "Wait a minute, Steve, there's someone I want you to meet."

"Not another one of your friends with the hots for me!" Steve groaned. "Jamie, you know that sort of thing never works out. They fall madly in love with me and then you get infuriated with me when I break things off."

"Don't worry. I've taken a vow never to introduce another friend of mine to you, no matter how much they might beg me to." She tugged on Steve's arm. "The person I want to introduce you to is my date, Rand Marshall. That's him, over there."

Steve stared at Rand, who was glowering at him. Then he grinned at his sister. "It's definitely *you* he has the hots for, Jamie. You want to know something hilarious? He thinks you and I have something going, I can tell. He looks as if he'd like to cut me up and use me for fish bait!" Steve laughed uproariously at the thought.

Rand's lips thinned. The other man's bold laughter was the last straw. He would not leave Jamie at the mercy of that smug, green peacock! He strode to her side, feeling possessive and protective and a host of other feelings, previously foreign to him. Nothing, not even the much-vaunted Marshall pride, could've kept him away from her.

"Rand, this is my brother Steve," Jamie blurted out the moment Rand joined them. His warlike expression alarmed her. "Steve, meet Rand Marshall."

It was an incredible anticlimax. "Your brother?" Rand echoed, and his combative anger was abruptly squelched, leaving him oddly bemused. "He's your notorious brother Steve?"

"The one and only." Steve smiled and held out his hand to shake. "So you're a new friend of Jamie's?" He eyed Rand speculatively. "You don't look like her usual sort of date."

"Don't say another word, Steve," Jamie said.

"What's her usual sort of date?" demanded Rand.

Steve laughed. "The well-trained, repressed type. And they inevitably bore her to death because she's so well-trained and repressed herself."

Rand gave a shout of laughter.

"Since you two are hitting it off so well together, why don't I just leave?" Jamie interjected coolly. Watching Rand with Steve reminded her that she'd spent all her dating years avoiding heartbreakers like her too-charming brother, only to end up falling for one at the supposedly wise age of twenty-five. Her pulses raced with anxiety. "I'm sure you'll have far more success stalking the *babes* without me around to inhibit you." She started to walk away.

Rand hooked an arm around her waist and pulled her to him. As she'd known he would? As she'd hoped he would? Jamie's head whirled with confusion.

"The only babe I intend to stalk tonight is you, Jamie," Rand drawled softly.

Steve applauded. "Nicely done." He pinched his sister's cheek. "It's refreshing to find you with a man you can't scare."

"I'd find it refreshing to find you with a woman you couldn't beguile and bamboozle with your phony charm," she told her brother severely.

Far from being affronted, Steve seemed delighted. "My baby sister," he said, patting her shoulder fondly. "Always haranguing me about my shallow life-style. She's my toughest critic, but I love her best of all."

"You realize, of course, that I've heard you say the same thing to Mom, Grandma, Cassie and Saran," Jamie said, unmoved by his claim of brotherly devotion.

Steve chuckled, then leaned toward Rand and lowered his voice conspiratorially. "You won't be able to beguile or bamboozle her, either, Marshall. I advise you not to try." He kissed Jamie's cheek, shook Rand's free hand and melted into the crowd.

Rand and Jamie faced each other uncertainly. "Steve said that you thought he and I were a couple," she remarked in an attempt to breech the lengthening tension-filled silence.

"He was wrong. I immediately saw the resemblance between you two and guessed he was your brother."

"Oh, sure." Jamie rolled her eyes. "That's why you were so incredulous when I told you who he was. You thought he was an old boyfriend of mine, and you were jealous." The notion pleased her immensely.

"As jealous as you were last night when I told you I was at Darby's with a date," he shot back.

"I can't believe it." Jamie heaved an impatient sigh. "We're starting to fight again. I argue with you more than I ever have with anybody, including Steve or Saran." She gave a confused laugh and shook her head.

"Don't you know why we fight so much?"

"Because we're obviously incompatible."

"Because we're so hot for each other we're burning up, but we haven't been able to act on it. Believe me, honey, there's nothing like sexual frustration to keep your temper at the boiling point."

"I should've seen that one coming," she said wryly. "If we're not fighting, we're talking about sex."

"I know a way to break the stalemate. Go to bed with me tonight, Jamie. That'll take care of the frustration and the fighting and the unremitting conversations about sex."

"You're saying that if I sleep with you, we'll be immediately transformed into compatible, congenial companions who'll have deep, meaningful discussions about things like music and literature and world affairs?" It was a laughable premise, and she did laugh, a little. "Do you really think I'm that gullible, Rand?"

"I was hoping you were. A man can dream, can't he?"

Her eyes sparkled with humor. "By all means, dream on." And then she grew serious and gazed at him, her expression earnest. "Rand, I overreacted when you tipped the man at the door. That fight wasn't about sex at all. It was a difference of opinion, and I'm sorry for condemning you."

He was taken completely off guard by the unexpected apology. It occurred to him that he'd spent little time talking things out in his usual dealings with women. He'd always believed that action—sexual action—was far more effective than words as a means of communication.

In the next instant, he realized that sex was also an effective way to avoid communication. His eyes widened. Good Lord, what was this? A flash of insight?

He stared at Jamie, who was watching him quizzically.

"You look thunderstruck," she observed. "Did my apology shock you that much?" Unlike Rand, she was experienced in talking things through; one couldn't live among the chatty Saracenis without acquiring communication skills.

"I guess I'm not sure what I'm supposed to say next." That was certainly true. Sex to avoid communication? Where were these thoughts coming from? And why was he having them here?

"Well, you could say something like 'I'm sorry, too, Jamie.' You could say 'I was trying to impress you. I didn't realize I'd come across as an arrogant elitist.'"

"An arrogant elitist?" He was indignant. "I am not!"

"I didn't say you were. I said you could say that you'd come across that way."

"Well, if I did, and I didn't, I guess I'm sorry."

"Such a heartfelt apology."

The tension between them had somehow dissipated. Suddenly, they were grinning at each other.

"Sometimes I can get overzealous and preachy," Jamie confessed, gazing at him from beneath her eyelashes. "And you're right, I do have a tendency to believe I'm right most of the time." Her blue eyes danced roguishly. "Maybe because I usually am?"

He chuckled appreciatively. "While I won't apologize for generously tipping the doorman, I admit that I shouldn't've bribed Saran for your phone number."

"Which you haven't used yet."

"I intend to remedy that and make full use of it."

"You don't really have to," she swiftly assured him. "The only phone in our house is right in the kitchen where everybody hangs out. And listening in on conversations is a favorite Saraceni pastime, especially when the TV programs break for commercials."

"I guess that means you won't talk dirty to me over the phone." He feigned disappointment. "Maybe I won't call after all."

They laughed, gazing warmly at each other.

"Now we're going to sing and we want everybody to join in," the jovial Irish tenor announced into the microphone, his brogue thick and melodious. Song sheets with the printed words to the songs were being passed out, and somebody thrust one into Jamie's hand.

"Oh, good, they're doing 'Clancy Lowered the Boom,'" she exclaimed as the band sounded the first notes.

"*We're* supposed to sing?" Rand looked less than pleased. He'd thought they would be entertained by the Irish singers and dancers, but he hadn't counted on having to take part in it himself.

Jamie sung along with the exuberant crowd, laughing when she missed a word or note. She might be cautious and controlled when it came to dating, but she had no reserve when it came to joining the crowd in song.

Rand shifted uncomfortably. He wasn't really the participant type; he much preferred observing. He'd always been a parallel type of person, not really engaging or involving himself with those around him—not even if it was the woman who happened to be sharing his bed.

Since childhood, perhaps in defense against his parents' alternating indifference and disapproval, he'd held himself apart from others. It wasn't until he had met Jamie that he'd felt this peculiar, inexplicable urge to get close, to abolish whatever obstacles—tangible or intangible—stood between them. He wanted to be close to her, and not just sexually. He wanted emotional intimacy, something he'd always been careful to avoid.

The term seemed to reverberate in his head. *Emotional intimacy?*

Rand broke out in a cold sweat. It was truly paralyzing, not to mention inconvenient, to be hit with a perceptive flash of insight in the middle of a barroom filled with people bellowing "Clancy Lowers the Boom."

What was going on here? he wondered frantically. He had never been the introspective type. But now his own thoughts were beginning to sound gleaned from one of those pop psychology books that proliferated the best-seller list.

"Come on, Rand. Sing along," Jamie urged, eyes sparkling.

He shook his head, preoccupied with the astonishing revelations being divulged there. He'd been accused of being commitment phobic by women who read those best-selling books about men who won't love. He'd accepted the diagnosis without turning a hair; sometimes he even used it as a convenient excuse for his behavior.

But true commitment phobes didn't hunger for the perils and pitfalls of emotional intimacy. The very thought would send them running. Rand gazed into Jamie's warm, laughing eyes and knew he wasn't going anywhere.

"You don't have to look so horror-stricken," Jamie teased, taking his hand. "You can't sing any worse than I do."

"Honey, what's going on in my head is truly horrifying. And it has nothing to do with singing."

Had she pressed him, he might have launched into his anticommitment diatribe, provoking another distancing fight between them. Instead, she joined in the next song.

The enthusiasm and infectious high spirits of the crowd were an antidote to brooding. Jamie wasn't going to fight with him, and after awhile Rand ended up singing after all. They drank some green beer, sampled the authentic corned beef and cabbage, sang some more and made a few riotous attempts to learn an Irish folk dance.

Sometime after midnight, the band segued into a set of slow, romantic ballads. After the hours of noisy revelry, couples were ready to dance, slow and quiet. So were Jamie and Rand. Neither had to say a word. Hand in hand, they moved to the dance floor.

Rand pulled her close and molded her against him, his big hands masterful. Jamie twined her arms around his neck with a soft sigh as the golden warmth spread through her. They swayed slowly, their movements in sync, as if they'd been partners for years.

One of his hands glided slowly along the length of her back to cup her nape. He massaged it sensuously, his fingers tangling in the gold clasp of her necklace from which the small gold shamrock dangled.

He liked the idea of her wearing the jewelry he had given her; it seemed a kind of symbolic branding, which marked her as exclusively his. Of course wedding rings traditionally served that purpose. The renegade thought popped into his head and quickly, in sheer self-defense, he banished it.

And concentrated on the intoxicating feel of her in his arms.

Hours later they parted at her front door after a long, passionate good-night kiss. It was nearly three a.m. and the small front porch was as illuminated as a turnpike toll-booth area, thanks to the incandescently brilliant porch light.

Rand shaded his eyes with his hand as he started down the front walk. On impulse, he turned around to find Jamie standing in the doorway, watching him.

"Do you—uh—want to do something tomorrow?" he asked, striving for a diffidence he was far from feeling.

"I promised Dad that I'd go to the beach with him and help Brandon and Timmy fly their new kites."

"Dare I suggest it? Change your plans. Let one of the other members of your pluralistic household fly kites with your daddy and the kids."

"There is no one else. Mom has some doll business, Cassie and Saran have to work at the mall, Steve is unavailable as usual, and Grandma isn't into kite flying. Dad can't help both kids at the same time—it really does take two adults."

"What about the boys' own father?" persisted Rand. "Doesn't he visit them on weekends? Let him take them."

"Oh, their father has visitation privileges." Jamie's mouth grew taut. "And two or three times a year he breezes in for a few hours, makes a lot of promises he doesn't keep and then takes off again. That's why I never break a promise I've made to Timmy and Brandon. Neither do Cassie or our folks. We want them to know that there are some people in this world who do keep their word."

"Very admirable." Rand was back on the porch step, within touching distance of her again. "But damned inconvenient for me. I suppose the only way I'll get to see you tomorrow is if I offer to come along and fly a kite?"

"I'd like to have you come, but I certainly don't expect you to," Jamie said quickly.

"And what's maddening is that you really mean it. This is no manipulative power play. You'll go whether I come along or not. Which puts the ball firmly in my court."

She smiled. "That's tennis. We're talking about kite flying."

"Which I haven't done for years."

"You probably don't *do* too many things. You have things done for you."

"You make it sound like I'm some kind of inactive slug!" Rand protested. "I get lots of exercise. I work out at the club, run, swim, play tennis and racquetball and even an occasional game of golf."

"Those are your male bonding activities," Jamie said knowledgeably. "And I'm not talking about exercise. I mean that you don't *do* anything with women except take them out for the occasional obligatory dinner, show or party. On the whole, if you're spending time with a woman, you're spending it in bed."

"I can assure you, that when I'm in bed with a woman, I'm definitely *doing* something. With her." He raised his brows suggestively. "Or to her."

Much to her annoyance, she felt herself beginning to blush. "I knew you'd say something like that. I hoped that you would restrain yourself, but of course you didn't."

"You think you know me so well," Rand growled. "Am I correct in assuming that you've gleaned all this knowledge about male bonding activities and sexual socializing from your infamous brother Steve?"

It was particularly aggravating that she'd so accurately depicted his life, or life-style, as the case may be. "What have you been doing all these years? Following your brother around, taking notes?"

"Just listening and observing and filing things away in my mind." Adding insult to injury, she glanced at her watch. "It's very late, Rand. Good night and thanks for tonight. It was fun."

"You already gave your perfunctory, polite little speech of dismissal. Right before I kissed you. It irritated me then and it irritates the hell out of me now."

"I'm going inside. You just want to start another quarrel."

"I just want to take you to bed and get you out of my system!"

He recoiled, appalled by his outburst. If she were to slam the door in his face and refuse to see him again, he knew it would be nothing less than he deserved.

But to his total incredulity, she laughed instead. "You're not supposed to come right out and announce your true intentions, Rand. You have to keep your hidden agenda artfully concealed, disguised under a barrage of calculating smooth talk. Careful, Rand, you're losing your cool. Steve would never make such a fatal slip."

It warmed her that Rand had. Having him express honest frustration, man to woman, was certainly preferable to being treated to insincere charm while being viewed as a sex object.

He stared at her, flummoxed, torn between wanting to laugh and wanting to strangle her. She was irrepressible. And relentlessly impertinent. And somehow she reached him on a level that no other woman ever had.

"You're such a...a—" Words failed him. Damn, if he were writing a similar scene as Brick Lawson, he would have no trouble coming up with just the right witty rejoinder or trenchant barb. But as Rand Marshall, living his life, suddenly he was dumbstruck.

"'Night, Rand," she called sweetly, turning to close the door.

"We're not ending the evening this way," he muttered. He had to reassert his dominance in this relationship. It was absolutely imperative. "Kiss me good night."

"But we already—"

He caught both her hands and jerked her toward him. "No arguing. Just do it."

Jamie stared up at him assessingly. He wasn't really angry, she decided thoughtfully. Rather, he seemed disconcerted and uneasy. He wanted her, though he didn't want to. A small smile tugged at the corners of her lips. How inconvenient for him! And he'd already made his feelings on inconveniences quite clear.

She felt the force of his gaze drawing her into him, bending her to his will, making her forget everything but the wonder and the magic she'd discovered in his arms. They'd had a wonderful time tonight, except when they'd been fighting, and even fighting with Rand was more interesting and exciting than doing anything else with anybody else. What she felt with him, for him, she'd never experienced before.

Her fingers crept up to trace the sensual outline of his mouth. Desire shuddered through her. He had such a gorgeous mouth. Tempting, sexy... She really wanted to kiss him, so very much.

"Rand," she whispered. Her arms slipped around his neck, and her body was soft and pliant against his. Her senses spinning, she lifted her mouth to his and touched his lips with hers.

And then they were kissing, deeply, wildly, as colors exploded inside her head like an internal fireworks display. His big hand slipped into the bodice of her dress and cupped her breast. She was warm and softly rounded, and he caressed her, circling the stiff crest with his thumb, until she was whimpering with pleasure.

Abruptly, without warning, he moved away from her. Jamie gulped for breath and leaned weakly against the doorjamb.

"Good night, Jamie." His eyes were glittering like polished jewels. He felt masterful, the powerful, conquering male. Her surrender had been absolute and unconditional. He'd proven to both of them that she was his, whenever he wanted.

Rand walked triumphantly to his car, leaving her gazing, troubled and bemused, at his retreating figure.

He paused as he opened the car door. "What time are you leaving for the beach tomorrow?"

"After church," she replied huskily. "Around noon."

"I'll see you then."

Her eyes widened. "You're coming with us?"

"I'll be here at twelve."

Jamie stood at the door, listening to the sound of his car roar along the quiet streets of Merlton. When silence descended once more, she flicked off the porch light and slipped inside.

She thought of him until she fell into a restless sleep, tossing and turning as she dreamed of a man with dark golden eyes whose skilled hands caressed her, learning her most intimate secrets, whose hard, sensual lips carried her to previously unimagined heights of pleasure.

She awoke, her skin flushed, her body throbbing, with Rand's name on her lips.

Nine

On Sunday afternoon Rand and Jamie drove to nearby Long Beach Island with her father and her nephews, Brandon and Timmy. They tramped onto the deserted beach with the two new red, yellow and blue kites. The requisite stiff breeze was present, but launching the kites took some skill and patience. Since Rand was around, Al Saraceni quickly opted to sit in a beach chair and read the Sunday paper.

Rand, remembering the kite-flying days of his youth, instructed the boys. "You don't run to get the kite into the air. You stand with your back to the wind and slowly let out some of the string."

He helped Timmy with one kite while Jamie and Brandon struggled with the other. When both kites were flying high, the two little boys took over.

"You know how to fly kites real good," an admiring Brandon told Rand.

"Our family chauffeur, Moses Scott, taught my brother and me how to fly them when we were about the same ages as you guys," said Rand with a smile of reminiscence.

"A what?" demanded Timmy.

"A chauffeur. It's someone who drives you places in the car," Jamie explained. "You have five of them—your mom, your grandparents, Saran and me."

Rand grinned at her explanation.

"Did your chauffeur wear a uniform?" Jamie asked curiously as they watched the boys run along the beach with the kites.

He nodded. "Moses was one of my favorite people when I was a kid. My brother and I were raised by the servants because our parents were never around. Lucky for me, I liked the servants better than my folks. A good thing because the servants liked me better than my folks did anyway."

Jamie slipped her hand into his. He was talking about a world she could barely imagine. It sounded so different from her life, so cold and sad. "Let's leave the kids with Dad and go for a walk," she suggested softly.

"You want to be alone with me." His mouth curved into a satisfied smile. "If I'd've known that the poor-little-rich-boy bit would work so effectively with you, I would have used it from day one."

Because she understood he was using flippancy to distance himself from her and from his less than idyllic childhood memories, she didn't retaliate. "I want to walk on the beach," she said mildly. "If you don't want to come, you can stay with the kids and I'll walk with Daddy."

"You're walking with me." He slipped a possessive arm around her shoulder. "Babe," he added in a perfect imitation of Steve Saraceni.

Leaving the children under their grandfather's watchful eye, Rand and Jamie set off for a long walk along the beach. It was cooler than yesterday's record breaker, the temperature just reaching sixty, and it was far too cold to wade in the surf, so they kept walking in the sand. For miles, talking and teasing and laughing, completely absorbed in each other.

Both were astonished to learn that it was nearly five o'clock when they finally returned to the spot where the boys, having tired of kite flying, were building a giant sand fort with their grandfather acting as consultant.

"I lost all track of the time," Rand said incredulously, realizing it was true. He hadn't glanced at his watch once during those hours with Jamie. It was a most unusual occurrence. He was usually protective of his time, guarding against demands and infringements on it.

Al Saraceni insisted that Rand stay for dinner with the family. Jamie tried to offer him a graceful way out, suggesting that he might have other plans for the evening, but her father would have none of it. Rand was having Sunday dinner with the Saracenis. There was absolutely no question about it.

"I wonder what would've happened if I really did have other plans for tonight?" Rand murmured to Jamie as they sat together in the backseat of Al's big blue Buick. The children sat in the front, reading comic books.

"I'm afraid you'd be eating with us no matter what. Daddy is determined to offer you hospitality. You made a tremendous hit with him today, playing with his grandsons."

"Even though I disappeared with his daughter for half the afternoon?" Rand murmured provocatively, inching closer. He caught her hand and held it in his, playing with her fingers. "For all he knows, I might've been off having my wicked way with you."

"On a windy beach in the middle of the day? Not with me! My father knows very well that proper, discreet, restrained Jamie would never do such a thing."

"I seem to recall a time in front of the library when proper, discreet, restrained Jamie was none of those things. In fact, you never are when you're in my arms."

No, she wasn't. Flushing, Jamie chewed her lower lip. The comment demanded a response, but what could she say? She disengaged her hand from his. "I should've known we couldn't spend a whole day without any sexual moves or innuendos from you," she whispered reprovingly.

He took her hand and refused to let it go. "You'd be disappointed if I didn't make a single play for you. You'd start to worry that I didn't want you anymore." He interlaced his fingers with hers and settled back against the seat, pulling her closer to him.

"I wouldn't be disappointed, I'd be relieved. And I wouldn't worry, either," she whispered.

"No? You're that sure of your appeal, huh?"

"No! Yes! I mean—" She shook her head and laughed in spite of herself. "You manage to twist things around so that any answer I give will be wrong. I do *not* consider myself the cutest little trick in shoe leather."

With her free hand, she gave him a playful punch. He caught that hand, effectively restraining her. Laughing, Jamie began to struggle, using her knee as a lever to free herself. When he moved lithely to pin down her legs with one of his own, she wriggled, trying to remember how she'd escaped Steve's wrestling holds when they'd been kids.

There was a major difference, however. She and Rand weren't kids, and he wasn't her brother. The sensations evoked by their movements were beginning to border on the erotic. And she didn't feel like struggling anymore, she felt like melting into him.

She looked into his eyes and saw awareness and desire burning there. Her whole body began to throb.

"So, Rand, you think the Flyers will beat the Rangers tomorrow night?" Al's voice boomed jovially from the front seat.

Jamie jerked convulsively, and Rand reluctantly let her go. Except for her right hand, which he kept firmly in his. "Proper, discreet and restrained?" he whispered in a voice so low she could hardly hear. "Not with me, honey." She blushed, and he leaned forward, raising his tone to hale masculine heartiness. "I think the Flyers are going to kick some butt, Al."

Chapter three in the *Guide to a Modern, Old-Fashioned Courtship* recommended that courting couples spend time together doing things. Rand thought back to the bad old days when his idea of spending time with a woman meant taking her to bed. He smiled wryly. Well, he'd known from their first date that wasn't going to be the case with Jamie.

She liked doing things. She liked dancing, swimming, roller-skating, ice-skating and even bowling. She liked to go to flea markets and movies, to the theater and the museum and the zoo in Philadelphia. She liked to ride bikes and to hike, to pick strawberries at local farms and then make ice cream to eat with them. She enjoyed cooking as well as eating out.

She and Rand did all those things during the weeks that followed, usually alone, but sometimes with various Saracenis or some of Jamie's friends. They even played a few games of miniature golf! He called her every night, even if he'd been with her earlier.

To avoid providing the rest of the Saracenis with entertainment during television commercial breaks, he bought her a phone and had a jack installed in her bedroom. There, she could talk to him privately, responding to his outrageous suggestions and innuendos without inhibitions.

She fielded them with humor and grace, sometimes indulging in a few provocative remarks of her own. Knowing that Rand wanted her and admitting her own attraction to him were no longer threatening to her. She was in love with him; she'd never been more certain of anything in her life.

Her initial reservations about becoming involved with him seemed ridiculous to her now, as did her fears that he was a smoothly operating heartbreaker cast from the same mold as brother Steve. She and Rand had an honest relationship based on mutual respect and trust. And love.

Her parents and grandmother, never noted for their sub-
tlety, were beginning to ask her about reserving the Sons of
Italy hall for a big wedding reception in the not too distant
future. Jamie managed to persuade them not to ask Rand
to set a date and fended off their eager questions and plans.
But she found herself leafing through the library's copies of
Brides magazine. Articles on travel, particularly ones fea-
turing favorite honeymoon spots, interested her as never
before. And she was more entranced than usual by the sight
of a baby in its mother's arms.

For though she and Rand had yet to discuss marriage,
Jamie was positive that their relationship was moving in that
direction. It had to be! She loved him so.

And she wanted him, as much as he wanted her. The
flame between them burned hotter and stronger than ever,
becoming even more intense as their relationship deepened.
They couldn't be together without touching. Whenever
possible, they held hands; he was quick to put his arm
around her shoulder or her waist or to pull her onto his lap.

They kissed often and impassionedly, but never within
proximity to a bedroom. Jamie had been to Rand's house
three times, accompanied each time by her nephews, who'd
demanded to come along to see Rand's kitten. Somebody
was always home at the Saraceni house, making intimacies
there impossible. And though some of their most torrid
kissing and petting occurred in the car, the contortions required for making love in a sports car seemed too ridiculous to contemplate at their ages.

At night, lying alone in her bed in the small pink and yellow bedroom she'd slept in since infancy, Jamie lay awake
for hours, twisting and turning restlessly, tormented by
sharp, sweet aches of need.

Rand, alone in his big water bed in the high-tech black
and white room, did his share of tossing and turning, too.
He took lots of cold showers and increased his daily exercise regime, hoping to exhaust himself into sleep.

He thought about Jamie, dreamed about her, wanted her more than he'd ever wanted a woman. He planned elaborate seductions and invented schemes to pressure her into his bed—and didn't enact any of them. For though he desperately wanted to make love to her, and his desperation and desire increased daily, he wanted her to come to him without doubt or anxiety, to give herself to him completely, without reservation. He'd grown to care for her, to like her too much, for it to be any other way between them.

The only cloud in their almost idyllic relationship involved work—or Rand's alleged lack of it. He didn't tell her that he spent his days creating the latest as yet untitled Brick Lawson thriller while she worked at the library. His book proposal had been accepted with his customary whopping advance check arriving by mail. But he continued to make joking references about enjoying the life of the idle rich while Jamie, who loved her job, tried to interest him in the concept of meaningful work.

It would have been an amusing conflict in a Brick Lawson tale, but Rand found his predicament less and less entertaining. All his life, he'd fought against being exactly what Jamie thought he was—an aimless dilettante living off his trust fund.

But how to tell her about his writing? Especially now, after all the time they'd spent together? Rand told himself that he was merely avoiding the fight they were certain to have due to his secrecy. But there was more at stake than simply a fight, and in the dark, lonely hours just before dawn, he would admit the truth to himself. He knew that she valued honesty, and he'd been less than honest with her. He was loathe to risk the possibility of her ending their relationship.

It was a humbling and alarming admission for a former feckless, unconcerned bachelor to make. For he'd finally admitted to himself that his end goal in courting Jamie wasn't to get her into his bed. He couldn't imagine his life without her in it and he would go to any lengths to make her happy. Was he in love with her?

He was asking himself that vital question one warm Friday evening in May as he was leaving to pick up Jamie for the Phillies-Pirates doubleheader at Veterans Stadium in Philadelphia.

He was pulling out of his driveway in the Jag when Saran pulled up beside him in Jamie's car. "Rand!" she called out the window. "Can I talk to you for a few minutes?" She hopped out of the car and came over to him.

"Is there something wrong? Where's Jamie?" he asked, tensing with apprehension as he climbed out of his car.

"She's at home waiting for you to pick her up for the game. This isn't about Jamie, it's about me. I'm in trouble, Rand," she announced dramatically. "And you're the only one who can help me."

"Oh God!" Rand groaned. "You're pregnant." He felt the color drain from his face.

"I am not!" Saran exclaimed indignantly.

Relief flowed through him, followed by irritation. "Well, what else was I to think? When a teenage girl says she's in trouble she—"

"I'm going to fail English, and if I do I won't graduate," Saran interrupted. "My English teacher says if I don't turn in a five thousand word essay on Charles Dickens' use of the color red as a symbol in *A Tale of Two Cities* by Tuesday, she's giving me an F. I'll have to take English in summer school to get my diploma and I can't because as soon as I'm eighteen, on July first, I'm leaving Merlton and moving to New York."

"So write the paper," advised Rand, starting to get back into his car. He was eager to see Jamie.

"I can't! I hate English and I hate *A Tale of Two Cities* and this paper is already two months overdue and—"

"Two months? No wonder your English teacher is mad. Look, I know that kind of essay can be a pain to write, but just sit down and make yourself do it."

"I was thinking that you would write it for me," Saran said slyly.

"Ha! Think again, sweetie. My English essay days are long past."

"But it'll be easy for you since you're a professional writer." She flashed a triumphant smile. "Brick Lawson."

Rand gasped. "You—you know?" he managed to choke.

"Since the night of the Merlton Spring Sing," she said proudly. "I got bored in the kitchen with Grandma while you and Jamie were necking in the other room so I went exploring. I found your office with your computer and all that Brick Lawson stuff." She tilted her head and studied him, her dark eyes intent. "What I couldn't figure out was why you didn't tell Jamie. But since you didn't, I didn't say anything, either."

"You figured you'd hang on to the information until the most opportune moment for blackmail presented itself," Rand surmised caustically. "That's the deal here, isn't it, Saran? If I write your paper, you won't tell Jamie about Brick Lawson."

Saran shrugged. "I wouldn't do it if I wasn't really desperate. But I am. And I promise I'll never breathe a word about you being Brick Lawson," she added, smiling sweetly. "Although I don't know why you think Jamie would mind. She loves books, and you write them. It's a perfect match."

"She doesn't like the kind of books I write, and I've waited so damn long to tell her that now it's nearly impossible. She'll accuse me of lying to her and—"

"Uh-oh," Saran cut in. "Lies freak Jamie out. She's, like, into the truth."

"I'm well aware of that." Rand scowled at her. "Oh, hell, I suppose this is exactly what I deserve. I bribed you, an impressionable kid, I haven't leveled with Jamie... blackmail is a natural consequence of all that dishonesty."

"You'll probably have to tell her sometime," said Saran, sighing. "But I hope it won't be now."

"Now isn't the right time," Rand muttered. If writing that odious paper bought him a little more time, so be it. "I'll tell her eventually, but not until . . . not until—"

"Not until when?" Saran asked curiously.

"That's none of your business, you conniving little criminal. I'll do the damn paper, and you keep your mouth shut."

"Rand, you're an angel! A livesaver! I'll be grateful to you forever and ever." Saran gave him a smacking kiss on the cheek, then dashed back to the car. "Have a good time tonight," she called gaily as she pulled out of the drive.

Rand tried not to snarl; he tried to think positively. After all, he could still wait for the ideal moment to break the Brick Lawson news to Jamie. He hadn't read Dickens in years; maybe he'd gain some fresh insights from the old English superstar for use in his own writing. And last but definitely not least, scheming little Saran would pass English, graduate from high school and leave Merlton—he hoped forever!

On that happy note, he left to pick up Jamie.

It was Memorial Day weekend, the weather was warm and springlike, and Rand had been commissioned to help Jamie plant some flowers in the beds in front of the Saraceni house. He'd never planted anything before, but Jamie said putting in flowers over Memorial Day weekend was a long-time tradition for her and Cassie and their mother. The Saraceni family had many traditions, and he rather liked that. He contrasted them to his own family, that group of disparate persons who shared nothing but the tiresome obligations of old money.

Families. Chapter four in the courtship book recommended meeting and getting to know each other's families, if it was possible. Rand certainly knew the Saracenis from weeks of spending time with them, but Jamie had yet to meet another Marshall.

He frowned. Yesterday in the mail he'd received an invitation from his parents to attend the tenth anniversary party they were giving for his brother, Dixon, and Dix's wife, Taylor Ann, set for the last weekend in June. Just for laughs, he'd brought along the formal engraved invitation, with nary a personal word on it, to show to Jamie. It contrasted dramatically with the latest Saraceni invitation, a warm, verbal one from Jamie's Aunt Rita to "come on over for Uncle Bob's birthday and bring as many friends as you want."

"Naturally, I'm not going to Dix and Taylor Ann's party," Rand told Jamie as he took a long swallow from the glass of iced tea he held.

They were taking a break from planting begonias, sitting together on the bench swing that hung from the roof of the small screened-in porch in back of the house.

Jamie studied the invitation, running her fingertip over the raised letters. "Why not?"

"Being around my brother is coma-inducing, and his wife is an insufferable snob. Actually, I'll be doing them all a favor if I don't show up, especially my parents. Having me around will ruin the party for them. We haven't seen each other in three years, and it's better that way for all concerned."

"But it's wonderful, having you around," Jamie said loyally. Her eyes were troubled. "This is the most you've ever talked about your family, Rand. I'd figured from the little you said about them that you weren't close, but you're actually—" she paused, searching for the right word "—estranged from them, aren't you?"

"I always have been, even when we lived together. My brother is the son of my parents' dreams, and as far as they're concerned, I turned out to be the son from hell. They've disapproved of me since I was a kid, but after I graduated from college and refused to lead the life they'd mapped out for me—you know, a window-dressing job on the board of the family foundation, the round of parties and hunts, wintering in Palm Beach—yes, winter is used as a verb in their circles—they made it very plain that I had no place among the Marshalls.''

He could tell by Jamie's stunned expression that she couldn't comprehend it. It was no wonder. No Saraceni cut another Saraceni loose, no matter what. ''Rand, are you sure they feel this way? Sometimes misunderstandings are blown out of proportion and each side—''

''It's sweet of you to want to play family therapist, honey, but it won't work in this case. My folks consider me an ungrateful, disloyal miscreant because I've always wanted to live my life differently. To them, the idea of my work is—''

''But you don't work.'' She stared at him. ''Do you?''

''I do some . . . writing. Business-type stuff. It's too complicated to explain, but it's the way I earn my living.'' Well, it was, wasn't it? And he did write about business, sometimes. Sort of. The hero in *Land of 1000 Vices* was an everyday businessman, wasn't he? ''I don't actually live off my trust fund, Jamie.''

Tell her, a chorus of voices inside his head screamed. Putting it off any longer was inexcusable; keeping it a secret was insane. But . . .

He thought back to Jamie's reaction to the Brick Lawson books on the first day they'd met in the library. She'd made no secret of her scorn and disapproval. His mouth twisted into a grim smile. It was ironic that the one woman he'd become seriously involved with should share his family's antipathy toward his work. While he'd become inured to his family's disdain and rejection, the thought of having to endure Jamie's made his blood run cold.

Worst of all was his lie by omission, by not revealing the truth from the beginning. A lie that had been compounded each day he'd concealed the truth from her. And if she were ever to find out about that damn paper he'd written two weeks ago for Saran . . . His temples began to throb with tension.

"You're in business?" Jamie looked puzzled. "But why didn't you tell me, Rand? All this time I've been trying to—"

"Convince me that I should be engaged in some kind of interesting or productive line of work," Rand finished for her. Tread lightly, he warned himself. "I enjoyed listening to you. You tried so hard to be subtle and discreet and you were neither."

"But—"

"I'll fill you in on all the details later," he said, "but right now I want to hear about that library summer program you were hoping to get started after school lets out next month. Have you given it any more thought?"

A few weeks ago, she'd mentioned the plans she'd drawn up for a library camp, a program for school-age children who would otherwise be alone during the summer while their parents worked. As he questioned her about it now, Rand leaned forward, his eyes intent with interest. Jamie basked in the concentrated warmth of his attention, letting him guide the conversation, responding to him, unaware that she was carefully being steered from a potentially explosive topic.

For the rest of the afternoon, he was successful in deflecting her questions about his newly announced, albeit vague, profession. But after the outdoor picnic dinner, as the rest of the Saracenis socialized merrily in the backyard, Jamie and Rand retreated to a quiet alcove in the hall and she returned to another subject he'd managed to avoid all day.

"Rand, I've been thinking about that invitation from your parents to your brother's anniversary party."

He frowned. "I'm not going to go, Jamie."

"Don't you think that maybe they're extending the proverbial olive branch, Rand? I think you should accept. Families shouldn't be enemies."

"We're not enemies, we're totally indifferent to each other."

"Would you go if I went with you?" Jamie dared to say. She knew it was a risk, but she had to take it. She loved Rand too much to stand by and not help to breach the distance between him and his family.

"You don't want to meet them, Jamie. My mother is so cold she could freeze fire, and my father and brother will completely ignore you. They have nothing to say to anybody who isn't—"

"I'm not afraid to meet them." She smiled reassuringly. "I'm a Saraceni, I can take whatever they might dish out and give it back if need be." Her smile faded. "Unless you don't think I'm good enough to meet the exalted Marshalls?"

"Don't be ridiculous!" The notion inflamed him. "Dammit, Jamie, I'd be proud to introduce you to them."

She looked at the floor and said nothing.

"Do you want me to prove it? I will if I have to. I'll tell them I'm coming to the party and bringing you. Of course, my mother will undoubtedly demand your name and address to send you your own invitation. She's extremely—correct."

"And I'll write her a polite reply, accepting her kind invitation." Jamie's eyes gleamed. "I can be correct, too, when the occasion demands."

Rand shook his head wryly. "Mother will be stunned. She assumes that I associate strictly with barbarians who are unfamiliar with the social graces."

Jamie put her arms around his waist and gazed at him, her eyes blazing with love and pride. "Your family doesn't know the Rand Marshall that I know. I think it's about time they met him."

"Jamie, it's not going to be that easy. We won't arrive in Virginia and find a warm, welcoming family, eager to make a brand-new start. That only happens in made-for-TV movies." Already, his body was responding to her nearness. He closed his arms around her and drew her close.

"We'll go and deal with whatever happens, good or bad," she said huskily, standing on tiptoe to lightly brush her lips along his. "I think you need someone to champion you in front of that family of yours. And I want to be your champion. I'll let them know that it's no longer tolerable for them to mistreat you."

"Ah, Jamie, you're so sweet." He stroked her back with his fingers, his hands firm and caressing. "So loyal." His hands swept over her hips, pressing her more intimately against him. He loved the idea of her being staunchly on his side.

Loyalty was something he seldom experienced, but he'd observed that it was a Saraceni trait, binding them to each other and remaining unshaken through even the fiercest arguments. At first Rand had found it amusing, then fascinating, and at last he'd given in and admitted to himself that he admired that fierce family loyalty. Which Jamie felt for him, too.

The knowledge touched him viscerally, releasing a surging tide of emotion that sparked his passion to even greater heights.

Jamie felt the hardness of his muscled body and quivered as the familiar heat warmed her. He covered her mouth with his, and excitement and need exploded through her. Their tongues met and stroked intimately. Moaning softly, she pressed closer to him, her hips undulating sinuously, her body straining for his. But she wasn't close enough. Every time they touched, every time they kissed, this restless, aching yearning within her grew more and more intense.

He lifted his mouth from hers, but held her tightly, his body pulsating with tension. "If I don't stop now, I'll carry you upstairs to your bedroom and take you right there in your own bed," he said in a rasping voice, harsh with need. "I want you so badly that not even a yard full of your relatives would restrain me."

Jamie clung to him, weak with unslaked passion. "It's almost unbearable," she whispered, "this waiting and wanting."

"Drop the almost. It *is* unbearable." He smoothed his hand over her thigh, feeling the warmth of her skin under the soft, worn denim of her jeans. "Come home with me, Jamie. Spend the rest of the weekend with me at my place."

He'd asked her before, too many times to count. And she'd always refused. He braced himself, waiting for yet another no. How much longer could he wait? he wondered grimly, knowing the answer even as he pondered the question. He would wait as long as he had to; he was too crazy about her to even think of seeking physical satisfaction with anybody else.

Her body was throbbing. He'd unbuttoned his shirt while working in the hot sun earlier, and her fingers tangled in the thick mat of dark hair on his chest. A fierce wave of love and longing surged through her. It was the strength of her love for him, combined with the desire and passion raging within her, that made it impossible to refuse him anything. There were no more doubts or fears; she loved him, trusted him, too. It was time.

"I want to come with you," she murmured softly. "But I—" She gazed up at him, blushing. "What'll we tell everybody? I can't just waltz out the door with my suitcase."

"Why not? I'll be right with you. Just call, 'See you on Monday' as we leave. My guess is that no one will say a word."

Ten

___

"You were wrong," Jamie said to Rand as he loaded her small suitcase into his car. "You said no one would say a word but Mom yelled, 'Have a good time.'"

"And your grandmother said, 'Drive carefully' and quoted the number of traffic fatalities predicted over the holiday weekend."

They chatted desultorily during the drive to Rand's house, their easy conversation belying the intensity vibrating between them.

Once they reached his home, Jamie felt as if she were in a dream, yet all her senses were heightened to excruciating levels of sensitivity when Rand picked her up and carried her and her small suitcase directly into his bedroom. She was achingly aware of the hard muscular feel of his arms under her thighs, of the rippling movement of his shoulders, of the enticing male scent of him.

When he kicked the bedroom door closed with his foot, she stared at him questioningly. "The cat," he explained dryly. "If I don't keep the door closed, he insists on sleeping on the bed. And living with Reebok has taught me something I'd never known before—that I hate sleeping with a cat."

"Me, too." Her voice was dreamy. It was impossible to think of cats when she was trembling with love and anticipation for Rand. Who would soon be her lover. Her first and only lover.

The cool, silver moonlight illuminated the bedroom, which was decorated in the same black and white functional minimalism as the living room. Jamie thought of the cozy country-style bedroom of her fantasies and smiled. This room was large and it even had a fireplace, albeit a black granite one with ridiculous fake logs made of black and white ceramic in its hearth. It wouldn't be difficult to turn this trendy eyesore into the warm, homey nest of her dreams.

The water bed came as a bit of a surprise. When Rand laid her on it, coming down beside her, the rolling waves startled her into sitting up, wide-eyed.

She bounced a little; she simply couldn't help herself. The aquatic mattress seemed to pitch and roll. Jamie giggled irrepressibly. "I've never been on one of these things before." She slapped her hand down hard and watched the undulating movement.

"Jamie!" Rand made a grab for her. An unsuccessful one.

She went jouncing across the bed, rocking back and forth to stimulate the water's movement, fascinated by the ebb and flow.

"You're not supposed to play *with* the bed," he said with mock exasperation. "You're supposed to play *on* it." This time he reached her and pressed her down on her back, into the thick down-quilted cover. "With me."

She smiled at him, her eyes teasing, as she stroked his cheek with her fingertips. "Sorry. I guess I got distracted by the novelty."

"Ouch! What a blow to my formerly oversize ego." Rand lowered himself on top of her. "When we're in bed together, I want to be the only thing that distracts you."

She felt her body adjust to his heavy male frame, the water mattress absorbing and distributing much of his weight. "Oh, Rand," she said on a husky sigh. "I can't believe we're really here together."

"You can't believe it?" He gave a laugh as he hugged her to him. "Honey, do you know how long I've waited for us to reach this stage of the courtship?"

"Chapter five," Jamie inserted.

"Yeah. I was beginning to worry that we'd be mired in chapters one through four for the rest of our natural lives."

"You never thought I'd ever do this?" Boldly, with a sexual confidence she'd never dreamed reserved, cautious Jamie Saraceni could possess, she slid her hand to the front of his jeans and pressed the straining fullness there.

He clenched his teeth and drew in a sharp breath, squeezing his eyes shut as reckless pleasure stabbed him. "Proper little Jamie," he breathed. "Who'd've ever dreamed it?"

Pleased with her success, she bravely caressed him through the heavy denim. "I never thought I'd do this, either," she said wondrously. "Oh, Rand, I love you. I love touching you. I'm not afraid at all!"

Rand exhaled a shuddering breath and forced himself to remove her hand. "Baby, you're making me crazy. I want us to go slow, to savor every minute. And if you keep that up . . ." He gave her a rueful smile. "It's been a long time, Jamie. I don't want things to be over before we even begin."

She nodded, sliding her arms around his neck. "Kiss me, Rand," she whispered.

"Oh, yes." His voice was rough and deep.

His mouth came down forcefully on hers, but she was ready and waiting for it. He thrust his tongue into her mouth and she welcomed it, closing her lips around it and sucking it deeper inside.

He had taught her to kiss like this, she thought, reveling in the wonderful carnality of it. Just as he had taught her everything else about arousal and excitement and the wondrous joys of physical pleasure. And tonight he would teach her the final mysteries of sex, and she would learn what it is to be a woman filled and satisfied by the man she loves.

She murmured his name between the hard, deep kisses and struggled with his shirt to slide her hands under it and feel the heated bare skin of his back. He wedged his thigh between hers, fitting her to him, sending shock waves of pleasure jolting through her. When he began to rhythmically press against her, she moaned softly and flexed her fingers, scoring his skin with her nails.

And then, slowly, he lifted himself away from her to prop himself on his elbow and gaze at her. Her eyes flew to his face. "Rand...." she began and tried to pull him down to her.

"We have too many clothes on," he said with a husky laugh. "It's time to get rid of them."

She was suddenly, heart-stoppingly shy. The thought of boldly shedding her clothes sent a shiver of apprehension through her. And then she thought about Rand and his clothes. Was she supposed to undress him? Before or after undressing herself? Jamie frowned, lamenting her inexperience.

"I want to undress you." Rand's deep, low voice instantly dissolved her dilemma. Jamie closed her eyes, weak with relief. She felt his fingers on the buttons of her blouse, undoing each one in order with maddening precision. When she dared to open her eyes, she found that he was smiling.

"You're teasing me!" she accused shakily.

"Your eyes were as round as saucers when I mentioned taking off our clothes. You looked like a scared little virgin." He laughed softly. "Not that I have any experience with virgins, scared or otherwise."

Jamie swallowed. "You prefer women with experience."

"It's fairer that way. I've never wanted to assume the re sponsibility of taking a woman's virginity. Or the obliga tions it might imply." Her blouse now unbuttoned, he stared hungrily at her breasts, which were straining beneath her lacy ivory camisole.

"I see." It was going to be harder to tell him than she'd thought, she decided nervously. One thing was certain; she was *not* going to play the tired cliché of scared virgin! Her cheeks flushed. She had too much pride to cast herself in that hapless role.

Gearing up her courage, she sat up and began to unbut ton his shirt. Her fears flew from her mind when she slipped his shirt from his shoulders and gazed upon the strong ex panse of his chest, of the enticing mat of wiry, dark hair. Shrugging out of her blouse, she moved into Rand's arms and they kissed and kissed. Deep, hot kisses. Sexy, wet, mind-shattering kisses.

They sank down onto the mattress and the undulation of the water took on a wholly new meaning for Jamie. It was a primitive, elemental rhythm, as old as time and powerful as nature.

She lifted up a little as he deftly swept the camisole over her head, exposing her beautifully shaped breasts, the rounded white softness, the dusky rose tips that were al ready aching and taut.

"You're beautiful," he breathed. He feathered her nip ples with his fingertips, and unable to resist, he took one rosy bud into his mouth.

Jamie gave a sharp cry and arched upward. She felt him lave her nipple with his tongue, circling the crest and the tip before finally drawing it deeply into his mouth to suck.

Waves of pleasure washed through her, making her feel deliciously languid, hot and weak. It was as if an invisible cord was connected to a place deep in her womb, for she felt the effects there, too, wild and throbbing, making her writhe and twist as the forceful pleasure snaked through her.

"You're so responsive, so sweet," Rand breathed, lifting his mouth to the other nipple. He smoothed one big hand over her belly and beneath the waistband of her jeans.

Jamie sucked in her stomach and whimpered as his hand traced the lacy waistband of her panties. "Let's take these off," he whispered seductively, and while she watched him dizzily, he stroked her jeans from her body, taking her underpants with them.

She lay before him, naked and flushed. His eyes swept over her, studying her and the rich sweet curves of her body. He lingered over her taut, rounded breasts, the small waist and womanly curve of her hips, the long, shapely legs and the alluring dark triangle lushly shadowing her femininity.

"Oh, baby, I want you so much." His voice was thick. He wished he could be more eloquent, but his gift for words seemed to have shorted out in the electrical fire storm sizzling between them.

Jamie watched as he struggled with his jeans, working them over his swollen manhood, then repeated the procedure with his briefs. She stared at him, her blue eyes wide. He looked very strong and very powerful.

Their eyes met and held for a long, silent moment before Rand lay beside her and took her in his arms. His hands learned the shape of her, caressing every curve, savoring the soft and supple texture of her skin.

Jamie responded with all the pent-up longings of her passionate nature. The sensations he was evoking were exquisite, making her aware of her own femininity in a whole new and thrilling way. She wanted to give and give to him, to surrender herself to the strength and power of his masculinity—and to the strength and power of her love for him.

Hesitantly, but curious and excited, she reached out to encircle the pulsing, hot shaft with her hand. Rand drew in a deep, ragged breath and moved his body in counterpoint with her hand. Jamie felt his control slip, watched him shudder with the pleasure she was giving him and felt a surge of feminine power she'd never dreamed she possessed. Tenderness flooded her in loving waves as she continued to caress him. He seemed vulnerable, so totally in her command, and love swelled within her.

"I love you," she whispered over and over. "Oh, Rand, I think I fell in love with you the first moment I saw you in the library. At first I tried to fight against it because I was scared of what you made me feel. Of how you made me feel. But now I know that I was born to be with you."

Her words touched him. One benefit derived from their courtship was that in knowing her as well as he did now, he knew that she said what she meant and meant what she said. She was in love with him, and the pleasure that filled him at the thought swelled his heart with a tenderness the force of which he had never before experienced.

"My darling," he murmured, using that term for the very first time. Not even as Brick Lawson had he allowed one of his heroes to call a woman his darling, because the term had always seemed too—too emotional, too fervent, too intimate for a Brick Lawson man. Just as it was too much of all those things for a Rand Marshall woman.

But Jamie wasn't a Rand Marshall woman, she was *the* woman. Rand Marshall's woman, his darling.

And because he wanted tonight, their first time together, to be perfect, for the first time ever, he decided that his own immediate pleasure was secondary to their mutual fulfillment. He reluctantly removed her hand.

"You're shooting my good intentions to hell, my sexy little temptress," he said thickly, hauling her arms above her head to manacle her wrists with one hand.

She wriggled and playfully tried to break free. "You're so strong! It feels like I'm caught in a handcuff," she exclaimed.

"I've got a pair in the drawer," drawled Rand. "We'll use them next time. The blindfold, too."

He laughed wickedly, and she joined in. "You're a devil, Rand Marshall," she accused, then kissed him lovingly, her actions belying her words.

"And you're an angel." He kissed her rapaciously, and her response was just as ardent. "A sexy, beautiful angel," he breathed.

She made a small, yearning sound as his hand moved between her thighs and gently caressed the velvety folds. One long finger tenderly explored the hot secrets of her body, penetrating the softness, sampling the wetness. Deeper. Higher.

"Jamie." His voice, husky and thick, held a puzzled note. He felt the slight resistance, and her body arched and jerked spasmodically. "Am I hurting you?"

"No." She shook her head vigorously. Her hands caressed him, her lips nibbled a path along the hard tanned column of his neck. How could she put into words her surprise and discovery of the excruciating heat waves of pleasure his stroking fingers evoked? There were no words lyrical enough, sexy enough....

"You didn't hurt me at all, Rand," she breathed softly, clinging to him. A fiery restlessness tore through her, and she arched herself against him in silent invitation. Though she blushed at the audacious things he was doing to her and the boldly wanton things he said, she knew she would die if he didn't continue.

Rand stared at her face, her half-closed eyes with the long, dark lashes fluttering, her lips parted as she softly moaned her pleasure. His blood surged hotly in his veins. Observing her pleasure, watching her uninhibited impassioned response to him was incredibly exciting and arousing, almost as good as experiencing his own satisfaction. It was a wholly new concept to him, taking pleasure in someone else's pleasure.

He knew he was a good lover technically, able to bring his partners to orgasm, but for the first time ever, he realized how detached and mechanical his lovemaking had been in the past. There had never been this intimate connection he felt with Jamie, this sweet interplay of giving and taking.

Until now, sex was a purely physical activity for him, with predictable cycles of tension and relief. With Jamie, it was so much more. An outpouring of tenderness, a surge of desire so intertwined with emotion and need he couldn't begin to separate them. She totally engaged him, body and spirit, mind and heart.

Under his watchful, passionate eyes, Jamie rapturously surrendered to the coiling spirals of sensation twisting deeper, tighter, under his intimate ministrations.

"Yes, baby, just let go." Rand's voice, husky and rough and sexy, rippled through her, its effects as physical as his caresses. "I want to see you, feel you..."

The exquisite, aching, throbbing waves of heat radiating through her reached flash point and exploded within her like a shower of sparks. Jamie cried Rand's name as she floated on the shimmering waves of ecstasy, and he held her tight, watching her with proud, possessive eyes.

She was his. Suddenly, it all seemed so simple, so inevitable. From the moment they'd met to this moment in the dark, quiet bedroom. Everything that had happened between them, the laughter and the fights, the kisses and the courtship, had all been a necessary part of the natural progression to the here and now, where they would consummate their relationship with all the love and passion that burned between them.

But first... "Jamie, are you protected? Or shall I take care of it?" he asked softly. He'd never been sexually irresponsible and he wasn't about to be now, not with his darling Jamie.

"I guess this time it'll have to be you." She gazed at him with love-drugged eyes. She was so new at this, she'd actually managed to forget all about such essential preliminaries. How lucky for her that Rand was so thoughtful.

Moments later, murmuring sexy, intimate love words, he positioned himself between her thighs and gave a steady, smooth thrust of his hips.

Jamie drew a sharp breath and clutched his shoulders.

"Jamie, relax, darling." He stared into the brilliant blue depths of her eyes. And then he knew. "You've never been with a man before, have you, Jamie?"

She smiled tremulously. "No. Is it—obvious? Am I doing something wrong?"

She was gazing up at him, her big eyes nervous and uncertain. Rand felt himself melt. "No, sweetheart, of course not. But you should've told me this is your first time."

"Would you still have wanted me if I had?" she whispered softly, remembering what he'd said about avoiding virgins and the responsibilities and obligations he felt were inherent in initiating them.

Rand was remembering, too. "What I said before... Jamie, that doesn't apply to you. What I feel for you..." He paused and tried again. "It's different with you, Jamie. The same old rules don't apply, they never have. How can I explain it?"

He gave his head a shake. He couldn't begin to put it into words. This was a writer? he silently berated himself.

She seemed to understand. Touching her mouth to his, she whispered warmly, "I love you, Rand. And I want you so much. Please, please make love to me."

She traced his nipple with her fingertips, then her lips, as she gently fondled the pulsing masculine hardness that throbbed hotly in her hand.

"Jamie!" He moaned her name, tangling his fingers through her hair. He drew her head to him. "Darling, are you sure?"

"Oh, yes," she said so fervently that they both laughed, soft, easy bedroom laughter that seemed to strengthen the bonds of intimacy.

They kissed avariciously, then he drove into her satin heat slowly, filling her, stretching her. The creamy warmth of her enveloped him tightly, smoothly. "You're perfect, Jamie. So sleek and soft and tight." He lay still, allowing her body to gradually adjust to the presence of his.

He was her first lover. His mind reeled right along with his senses, which were already whirling with primitive sensuality. Everything she experienced with him would be new; her responses, her pleasure, everything. Instead of appalling him, the realization delighted him.

"I never dreamed it could be like this," Jamie whispered, moving her hands over the hard, broad expanse of his back. "Rand, you're inside me!" The knowledge was awe-inspiring; the feelings profound.

"You feel so wonderful," he gasped. "Like you were specifically, specially created just for me. Only for me," he added possessively.

"I was, I am," she murmured breathlessly. "Just as you're made for me." For he was, she was certain of that. It had been a long wait for her dream man to arrive in her life, but he had. He was here now, holding her, loving her. "Rand," she said, sighing.

And then he began to move, slowly at first, but with a steady, primal rhythm that made her whimper with dizzying pleasure. Obeying ancient feminine instincts that guided her, Jamie began to move in tandem, matching his rhythm with a complementing one of her own, tightening her small inner muscles around him.

Between them, they generated an explosive heat that hurled them into a hot whirlwind of passion, spinning them up to the sweet planes of rapture. And then, insensate with bliss, they drifted slowly down to the languid, sated seas of satisfaction.

Again and again during the long, passionate night they made love, reaching for each other in an erotic cycle of arousal and passion, satisfaction and sleep. And each revolving spiral of desire and fulfillment strengthened the powerful sexual bonds between them.

It was nearly noon when an incessant pounding on the door roused Rand from the deep sleep that had claimed him after an intense, early morning session of lovemaking sev-

eral hours before. For a few minutes he lay in a mindless
stupor, unable to even contemplate moving from the bed.

Curled up next to him was Jamie, one slim leg curved
around his, her arm flung over his chest in possession and
trust. She was sleeping soundly, her lips slightly parted, her
chest rising and falling softly, matching the rhythm of her
slow, even breathing.

A rush of affection mixed with desire surged through him.
She was so sweet, so beautiful, he thought, gazing at her.
Her hair was tousled, and the sheet was pulled to her chin.
He smiled, wondering how she could manage to simulta-
neously look so young and innocent and yet so alluring.

When the pounding at the door ceased, he sighed with
relief and prepared to settle back to sleep. Only to have the
doorbell begin to ring.

Cursing to himself, Rand climbed out of bed, careful not
to disturb Jamie, who hadn't even stirred. Poor baby, he
had really worn her out—but she had been as eager as he, he
reminded himself. She'd initiated their lovemaking at dawn,
just as the first rays of sunlight were filtering through the
cracks in the black and white blinds. He remembered being
awakened by her soft mouth and her caressing hands, and
his body began to grow taut in recall.

The doorbell continued to ring, and he wanted Jamie to
rest, so he snatched his white terry-cloth robe from the Lucite hook in the bathroom, belted it and padded swiftly to
the front door. He half-expected to see some eager children
hawking the latest sales item from their school, scout troop
or sports team. In this neighborhood he'd learned that
someone under twelve was always selling something.

Reebok rubbed against his ankles, meowing and purring
at the same time. "Okay, pal, I'll get your breakfast in a
second." Rand bent to stroke the small cat's head. "First let
me buy whatever cookies or raffle tickets or magazines it'll
take to send the little pests on their way."

He was astonished to find Daniel Wilcox at his door.

"Sorry, did I wake you?" The words were spoken automatically and without even a hint of regret.

"You made enough racket to wake the dead!" Rand growled. "What are you here for?"

"I've been calling all morning and kept getting a busy signal," Daniel said testily.

"That's because my phone is off the hook. I didn't want to take any calls this morning."

Daniel chose not to respond to that. "Well, I thought I'd take a chance and come by. I have two tickets to the Phillies' game tonight and wondered if you'd care to join me?"

"I have a date, but thanks anyway."

"With Jamie Saraceni?" Daniel laughed shortly. "Lately, you seem to have a standing date with her."

Rand didn't feel like discussing his relationship with Jamie, particularly not with Daniel Wilcox. So he shrugged and changed the subject. "How come *you* don't have a date tonight, Dan? It's a holiday weekend, and you always have big plans for any holiday. It's practically an indisputable law of nature."

"Not any more," grumbled Daniel. "My social life hasn't been too terrific lately. I'm in a slump." He scowled. "I don't understand it. Not even Mary Jane Strayer will go out with me. She claims she's dating another guy steadily now."

"Why don't you give your hygienist—what's her name? Angela?—a call?" Rand suggested. He was feeling benevolent toward the whole world today, even to the point of playing matchmaker.

"Angela?" Daniel gasped. "You mean me, date Angela Kelso? You can't be serious!"

In the bedroom, Jamie came slowly awake, stretching and reaching for Rand. She was naked beneath the soft, silky black and white sheets, and felt languid and sexy and wonderfully voluptuous.

To her disappointment, Rand wasn't in bed. He wasn't even in the room. Her eyes fell on the clock and she gasped softly. Ten after twelve! She was shocked. It couldn't be; she'd never slept so late in her entire life.

And then her lips curved into an irrepressible smile. She was entitled to stay abed until noon. After all, she'd spent most of last night doing, saying and feeling things she never had in her entire life.

Now fully awake, she felt charged with a marvelous energy and starved for breakfast. Hopping out of bed, she spied her clothes scattered on the floor and blushed. There was her blouse, over there was her camisole, and tangled in a heap at the foot of the bed were her jeans and panties. One shoe was over by the door, the other one halfway across the room.

Unwilling to get dressed without a shower, she peeked in Rand's big walk-in closet and found a black silk robe to put on. It hung to mid-calf on her, and she belted it tightly and headed out of the bedroom. She heard the sound of voices and figured that Rand had turned the television on, a natural thought for a Saraceni who lived with a TV going eighteen hours a day.

But then she ascertained that Rand was speaking to someone and she realized that he was either on the phone or—horrors!—talking to a visitor. She came to a dead halt, clutching the lapels of the robe around her. Peering around the corner, she could see Rand standing in the doorway... with Daniel Wilcox!

What was he doing here? She almost asked aloud, so great was her shock at the sight of Daniel Wilcox. She didn't think he was friendly enough with Rand to drop in uninvited. During the months she and Rand had been dating, they'd only seen him once, at Darby's, the night of Angela's birthday.

"I have the first three weekends in August, and you're entitled to one of them since you won part one of our bet," she could hear Daniel saying.

Their voices carried quite clearly to her place in the hallway, and Jamie stood frozen, unwilling to call attention to herself. She frantically hoped that Daniel Wilcox would wrap up his visit and go!

"So which weekend do you want, Marsh? Or do you have to consult with *Jamie* before you dare to express a preference?"

Jamie frowned at the definitely mocking inflection. She wished that Rand would send Wilcox on his way as swiftly and as rudely as possible!

But Rand didn't seem to take offense at Daniel Wilcox's presence or his snidely caustic tones. He merely shrugged and made no reply.

"You aren't going to try to claim the place for the Fourth of July weekend, are you?" Daniel demanded petulantly. "It's the biggest weekend at the shore all summer, and I've already made plans to throw a party, the likes of which you haven't seen . . . since my last Fourth of July blast."

"Relax, Daniel. The place is yours."

"You're releasing me from the terms of part two of our bet? Or haven't you won it yet?"

"Wilcox, for God's sake, will you shut up!"

"What am I saying? Of course you won the bet! No woman spends as much time with Rand Marshall as Little Miss Saraceni has without climbing into his bed." Daniel snickered. "So how was she, Marshall? The least you can do is to let me experience her vicariously."

Jamie felt the color drain from her face. It took only seconds for her to piece together their conversation and come up with the horrifying conclusion.

A bet? She felt as if she was being stabbed in the heart, so physical was the pain that gripped her. Rand had a bet with this cretin about getting her into bed? She wanted to deny it, but her mind was too quick and too reality-oriented to allow her that luxury. She'd heard Daniel Wilcox say it with her own ears.

Just as she hadn't heard Rand issue a denial. If it wasn't true, wouldn't Rand have been angered, or at the very least, puzzled by the other man's aspersions? Wouldn't he have uttered those saving words, "I don't know what you're talking about"?

But he hadn't said them because he'd made the reprehensible bet! Something about winning Wilcox's condo at the shore for the Fourth of July weekend if Rand Marshall took Jamie Saraceni to bed. Which he'd done, with resounding success.

She'd given her virginity to a man who'd taken her to bed on a bet! Jamie felt sick. Her next impulse was to hide, like a cat who's been hurt and seeks solitude to tend to its wounds. But she couldn't hide anywhere here; she had to get away. Now. And after she did she would never see Rand Marshall again. She'd never even say his name again.

Her eyes filled with tears, and she choked back a sob. Life without him stretched bleakly before her, all the emptiness and loneliness of missing everything that she had found with him. She would never laugh with him, never hug him or kiss him or make love to him again. There would be no more special smiles and private jokes.

Her mind seemed to splinter under the impact of the pain, the worst she'd ever felt in her life. So this was what rejection and deception felt like. For the first time she fully understood those brothers who'd come to her seeking vengeance for the hurt Steve's cavalier rejections had caused their sisters. Watching a loved one suffer this pain would fuel every primitive instinct for revenge.

Jamie shivered, remembering the dark days of her sister Cassie's divorce and how badly she'd felt that her sister was hurting. But she knew now that she hadn't a clue as to the true depth of her sister's suffering. Secondhand, the pain had been bad enough but this...*this* was firsthand and it was unbearable, a black despair that smashed her heart and shook the foundations of her very soul.

Jamie thought of how determined and how careful she'd always been to avoid romantic pain and suffering. How foolish and prideful she'd been to think that she could live and love without being hurt!

The pain built to an intolerable level, and Jamie couldn't endure standing passively for another minute. Taking action, any kind of action, was an absolute necessity.

She meant to run into the bedroom to grab her clothes and make her escape. But when she was halfway there, Jamie turned around and blindly, impetuously rushed into the living room.

Eleven

I think you should claim your prize, Rand," Jamie said coolly. She wished her voice wasn't quite so shaky and drew in a deep breath to steady herself. "After all, you earned it. You won. By all means, go for the fourth."

Rand and Daniel stared at her speechlessly. And in the silent moments following, as Rand continued to study her, his stomach began to churn. Her face was pale and her mouth set in a tight, straight line; her huge blue eyes were dilated and round. She was clenching her fists so tightly that her knuckles were splotched white. She was the picture of suppressed fury and pain held together by steely self-control.

She wasn't dismissing Daniel's talk of a bet with the sardonic contempt it deserved, Rand knew, feeling a sickening sense of doom descend over him. She'd taken it seriously!

"Jamie." Rand started toward her. "Sweetheart, I can explain." She backed away from him as part of him had known she would. He nearly groaned aloud. "Jamie, surely you can't believe that I would make such a bet—"

"I don't want to believe it." Tears were burning in her eyes, but by holding herself taut and rigid, she was able to keep them at bay. A fierce pride enabled her to succeed. She would not cry in front of these monsters! "Just like I didn't want to believe that Eric Crenshaw and Richard Aldero would try to use me for revenge because Steve dumped their sisters."

Rand felt panic grip him. He'd forgotten about those two clowns who'd tried to avenge their sisters' rejection by Steve Saraceni by romancing and rejecting Jamie. Although they hadn't succeeded, their very attempts, along with her brother's checkered romantic history, made the idea of an exploitative bet between men credible to her.

"At least Eric Crenshaw and Richard Aldero told the truth when I put the facts to them. They didn't try to carry the deception any farther." A searing anger, coupled with an equally intense hurt, almost toppled her control. But she bravely, stubbornly managed to hold on to it. "I never thought I'd end up using those two sleazeballs as examples of honesty and integrity. But you make them look like Eagle Scouts."

"Look, I'd better leave." Daniel Wilcox spoke for the first time since Jamie's appearance. He looked distinctly uncomfortable, keeping his eyes fixed firmly to the ground and shifting uneasily from one foot to the other.

"You're not going anywhere until you tell Jamie that there was never any damn bet concerning her and me!" Rand snapped.

Daniel cleared his throat. "I really don't want to get involved—"

"You're already involved, you idiot!" Rand advanced on him, grabbing a handful of Daniel's pastel striped polo shirt. "You're responsible for this entire misunderstanding! The least you can do is to—"

"Lie for you?" Jamie inserted acidly. "Don't bother, Dr. Wilcox. I won't believe you anyway."

Rand let go of Daniel to turn to Jamie. His eyes were a dark, flaming amber. "And what does that say about your true opinion of me, Jamie?" Sheer unadulterated rage began to replace his dizzying sense of panic. "You said that you loved me but the minute you heard something that could be misconstrued as negative, you did one hell of an about-face and started flinging accusations."

"Could be misconstrued as negative?" Jamie echoed. "Now there's a tidy euphemism for your cold-blooded, egomaniacal, dehumanizing bet!"

"I have to agree that she has a point about owning up to the facts instead of fostering the deception, Rand," Daniel inserted earnestly. "It's like throwing good money after bad. Better to cut your losses and—"

"You're the last person in the world to be moralizing, Wilcox!" roared Rand. "Now, will you kindly tell Jamie that I never agreed to any bet!"

Daniel grimaced. "All I know is that shortly after I offered you my condo at the shore for a weekend if you managed to get a date with her, you told me that you were taking her out."

"I never took you seriously for an instant! I had a date with Jamie before you even mentioned your stupid condo! And I never agreed to—"

"I've heard enough," Jamie cut in. She couldn't stand here listening to this for another minute or she really was going to break down. Her control was slipping fast. "I'm leaving now. I'll call home and ask Saran or Cassie to pick me up." There was no way she could face her parents or Grandma just yet. She prayed they wouldn't answer the phone when she called.

"I'll take you home after we've talked this out," Rand said with chilling finality.

"No!" She couldn't bear to listen to any more of his lies, and the idea of being alone with him was too alarming to be borne. What if he tried to make love to her? A shiver rippled along her spine. Could she trust herself to resist him? Those long, passionate hours in his bed last night had given him a powerful weapon over her. Could she withstand the force of her own love for him should he decide to seduce her into doubting what she'd heard?

"There's no reason to talk, there's nothing more to say." Her blood was roaring in her ears, and she felt both burning hot and freezing cold. "You used me. I can't trust you, Rand Marshall. And without trust—there's nothing." Her voice was bleak and flat.

"I *used* you? That's rich!" He gave a harsh, mirthless laugh. "When we first met, I was determined to get you into bed and if I'd succeeded then, maybe your accusations would be valid. But that's not what happened."

Rand began to pace the floor with the manic energy of a caged wild animal. "For months, I've played it your way. The old-fashioned courtship. All those dates! Those endless nights when I thought I'd explode from frustration because I was respecting your wishes not to hustle you into bed. And, don't kid yourself, I could've gotten you there before last night, baby. You've been ready for it, you've been wanting me for weeks. Months!" he added with a flourish. "But, no, I played by the rules you set, breaking all my own, because... because—"

He broke off as the realization struck him with full force. Because he was in love with her. He loved her and wanted to please her, to make her happy, even if that meant circumventing his own needs and pleasure to place hers first.

"Last night?" Daniel stared from Rand to Jamie, his face reddening. "Do you mean last night was the first time that you—" He pulled a handkerchief from his pants pocket and wiped his brow. "Oh, boy, I sure screwed things up by showing up here today, didn't I?"

For just a moment, Rand's and Jamie's eyes met and memories of last night passed, almost tangibly, between them. But then Jamie pulled her gaze from his and turned pointedly to Daniel. "I suppose I should be grateful that you arrived when you did. Before—" She swallowed hard.

Before what? her heart cried. Before she'd fallen in love with him? She already had, ages ago. Before she slept with him? Another moot point.

Clutching the lapels of the robe tightly, protectively around her, she whirled away from Rand's searching eyes and Daniel's guilty ones and ran from the room.

"Jamie!" Rand called after her. He restrained himself from going after her. As upset as she was, they might both end up saying things they didn't mean. He'd let her take a shower and get dressed; then he would talk to her. And she would listen to him, he'd make sure of that. They would clear up this unfortunate misunderstanding and put it behind them. Then he would tell her that he loved her.

"Look, Rand, I really am sorry about this," mumbled Daniel. "But I did make that bet with you. In Darby's, the night we were with Shelli and Maxi. Do you honestly not remember?"

Rand stared at his old friend and knew that their friendship, as they'd known it through the years, was over. Daniel had hurt Jamie, unwittingly perhaps, but he'd done it, just as he'd caused this terrible rift on a day that should have been a joyful, loving one for the pair of new lovers. Rand thought of the hurt, haunted look of betrayal in Jamie's eyes, and a spasm of pain ripped through him.

"You might've made a bet with me, but it was wholly one-sided. I never made a bet with you, a fact you deliberately neglected to tell Jamie," Rand said coldly. "Now get out of here before I give in to the temptation to knock your teeth down your throat."

Wilcox, always meticulous in matters of his own self-preservation, wisely chose to make a speedy exit.

From the bedroom, Rand heard the water in the shower running, and he resisted the almost overwhelming temptation to join Jamie there. She would be naked and wet and vulnerable, and he would pull her into his arms and clamp his mouth over hers before she could utter a single syllable of protest. It was certainly the way a Brick Lawson hero would handle a recalcitrant female.

Sighing heavily, Rand went into the kitchen to feed the cat instead. Jamie was not, nor had she ever been, a Brick Lawson heroine, one of those soft-headed, malleable little twits who probably only exist in male adventure novelists' and their readers' fantasies.

Jamie was stubborn, strong-willed and opinionated. She was funny, affectionate and complex; he found her endlessly fascinating. She interested him in a way no other woman ever had or could. He was in love with her, Rand admitted again. He couldn't wait to tell her so.

He visualized her as she had been last night in bed, passionate and vibrant, remembering her soft, sweet cries as he took her from virgin to lover. His breathing thickened. Just thinking about it, about her was having a lusty physical effect upon him. He wanted her so much, he couldn't imagine the day when he wouldn't.

He was so engrossed in his thoughts that he didn't hear Jamie emerge from the bedroom, especially as she was careful to tiptoe quietly down the hall to the front door. She had called Saran before taking refuge in the shower, and with any luck, her cousin should arrive just as she was ready to leave.

Her luck, however, seemed to have taken an appalling turn for the worse this morning, Jamie thought despairingly as she pulled open the front door. Saran wasn't outside waiting for her, and the creaking sound of the door had alerted Rand in the kitchen.

He shot into the living room just in time to see her slip out the door. "Jamie! Come back here!" His voice was sharper than he'd intended. But the sight of her stealthy departure had thoroughly disconcerted him.

She didn't stop, and he had to follow her outside, still in his robe and bare feet. He caught her arm and held her fast. "You're not going anywhere."

"I refuse to spend another minute with you."

"You've been crying," he said, taking in her puffy, red-rimmed eyes. She must've been crying in the shower, where the sound of the running water would muffle her sobs. Remorse flickered in his eyes. "Jamie, I'm sorry you were hurt by what Wilcox said. But regardless of what he claims, I never made a bet with him concerning you."

Jamie gulped. "He certainly seems to think you did. Are you calling him a liar? Saying that he made the whole thing up?"

"I remember him making some sort of stupid wager at Darby's the night of Angela's birthday. But I never took him up on it, Jamie. I didn't give it another thought until this morning when he showed up and started ranting on about it."

She stared at him, desperately wanting to believe him. Needing to believe him. She was in love with him; she wanted to think that last night's lovemaking marked the beginning of a permanent relationship between them, not the end of a one-sided deception.

Sensing her indecision and flickering hope, he cupped her shoulders with his hands and faced her squarely. "You spoke earlier about trust," he said quietly. "It works both ways, Jamie. Haven't the past months been about learning to know and trust each other? And if you trust me, you'll know that I wouldn't hurt you or use you."

Jamie began to cry. It was all too much, the dizzying heights and crashing depths of emotion she'd experienced since awakening less than an hour ago. She was about to let Rand take her into his arms, where she would melt against him and enjoy the supreme pleasure of being comforted by the man she loved, when Saran pulled Jamie's car into the driveway and lurched to a stop.

"Oh, no!" Rand groaned.

"I called her before I went into the shower and told her to come over right away," Jamie confessed tearfully. "Oh, Rand, I—"

"What's going on?" Saran called as she jumped out of the car. She dashed to Jamie's side, took in her tear-streaked face and Rand's tense one and arrived at her own conclusion. "Oh, no! Jamie found out about Brick Lawson! Oh, jeez, this is terrible. Don't be too mad at him, Jamie, he—"

"Saran!" Rand's voice was more of a bark.

Jamie took a few steps backward to glance puzzledly, warily, from Saran to Rand. "Brick Lawson? The writer?" she said carefully.

"Rand can explain everything," Saran inserted hastily, then proceeded to explain things on her own. "It's just that he knew you'd never go out with him 'cause you think Brick Lawson is a sleazy hack who writes porno trash and then he didn't tell you because he hadn't told you in the first place and we all know what an honesty freak you are." She stopped to gasp for breath.

"Rand is Brick Lawson," Jamie said flatly. She stared at Rand, stunned, her blue eyes wide and disbelieving. "The author of *Assignment: Jailbait*, *Land of 1000 Vices*, *Life is a Game of Craps* and *Untamed Bikers: Hard as They Come*. Are there any I've missed? It's true, isn't it, Rand? And Saran has known all along?"

Rand opened his mouth to speak, but Saran beat him to it. "Since we went to his house the night of the Merlton Spring Sing," she said rather proudly. "But I didn't tell him I knew until I needed a passing grade on my English theme. You know, Rand's really a good writer, Jamie," the young woman added ingenuously. "My English teacher even said so, sort of. After she read the paper he wrote for me for English, she said, 'Saran, you should be ashamed of yourself for hiding your light under a bushel all year. You have definite writing talent, and if you stick with it, you could be a professional writer someday.' She gave the paper an A, Jamie! Thanks to good old Brick here I'm going to pass English and will graduate with my class!"

"Good old Brick," Jamie said in a chilling tone. "May I assume that you blackmailed him into writing the paper, Saran? Told him that you'd tell me about his secret identity if he didn't?"

Saran nodded. "I know I probably shouldn't't've, Jamie, but I was desperate!"

"No, Saran, you were lazy." Jamie's eyes burned like twin flames. "You didn't want to take the time and effort to do the paper so you found someone to do it for you. You were dishonest, you cheated and you lied and you should be ashamed of yourself!"

"Well, I'm not." Saran shrugged, undaunted. "I'm just glad I'm going to pass English. And I think you should tell Rand that you're sorry for thinking his books stink. Lots of people like them and buy them. Someday I might even read one."

"Saran, I think you've said enough for now," Rand said, his eyes never leaving Jamie's face. "Why don't you drive home and Jamie and I will—"

"We're both leaving now." Jamie took the car keys Saran was dangling and stalked to the driver's side of the car.

"I want you to stay, Jamie," Rand said with quiet intensity.

"So you can spin some more lies?" she cried. "Oh, you are good at it, Rand Marshall! No wonder you're such a successful writer, you make the most implausible tales of fiction seem believable!"

"Name one implausible tale of fiction I've told you," snapped Rand. Her anger sparked his, and his temper flared. What a positively hellish day this had turned into! First Wilcox and the bet, and now, just as he and Jamie had reached an understanding about that, along came Saran and the Brick Lawson revelation.

His rage faded as quickly as it had come, leaving him feeling drained and depressed. The timing couldn't have been worse, he conceded gloomily. Having just spent their first night together, Jamie needed his love and attention and reassurance, but instead she was hit by lies and partial truths and subterfuge.

He knew how hard she would take it; he understood her just as she understood him. They were good for each other, they were good together, although one look at her taut, white face and he knew Jamie wasn't about to admit that right now. She was, paradoxically, emotional and cautious, passionate and controlled. And every single, contradictory aspect of her nature was working against him right now.

Tears swam in Jamie's eyes. "I'm not going to prolong this farce any longer." Her lower lip was quivering ominously; if she didn't leave immediately, she was going to burst into tears again, and she just couldn't let *him* see her crying over him. "Get into the car, Saran. We're going home," she ordered fiercely.

"Oh, Jamie, why don't you stay here and make up with Rand?" Saran said with a world-weary sigh. "You know you want to. You're madly in love with him, and everybody knows it."

"I can't expect a—a conniving little blackmailer like you to understand what truth and honesty mean in a relationship, Saran," Jamie said tightly. "Without them, there is no relationship, only self-delusion, and I've been suffering from an acute case of it lately."

Saran folded her arms in front of her chest and glared from Jamie to Rand. "Come on, Rand. Are you just going to let her go? She's dumping you, in case you don't know it. Don't let her do it. Pick her up and carry her into the house, and I'll be glad to take the car for the rest of the weekend."

"Forcible seduction isn't my style, Saran," Rand growled. "If Jamie wants me—"

"I don't!" Jamie interrupted hotly. "Now get into the car immediately, Saran. I'm going home, and I'm not about to leave an underage woman alone with the creator of *Assignment: Jailbait*."

Rand's golden eyes glittered and his mouth twisted into a grim line, but he said nothing.

Jamie glared at him, then opened the car door. He was standing where the stone path to the front door met the driveway, and he made no attempts to stop her from leaving. She told herself she was glad.

"I never want to see you again," she added, flinging the words at him. "Don't even try to call me because I won't talk to you."

Still Rand remained where he was, his face a tightly controlled mask. A mask that was concealing what? she wondered miserably. She felt lost, confused and utterly without direction. "Of course, I won't be going to Virginia with you for the anniversary party," she added, watching him. "I won't go anywhere with you, ever again!"

His only response was silence, a silence that spoke volumes to Jamie. She remembered how persistent he'd been in the beginning of their relationship, never taking no for an answer from her, pursuing her despite her reluctance and withdrawal. It was in marked contrast to his passive acceptance of her leave-taking now.

Was it because he'd finally achieved his goal and taken her to bed? She thought about the bet he had denied making with that odious Daniel Wilcox. Maybe he hadn't actually made a bet, but was it possible that her main appeal to him had been her sexual unavailability? Which had ended last night in his bed. Oh, she'd been available last night, all right! Every time he had reached for her, she'd been ready and willing. And at dawn, she had awakened, her body throbbing and sensitized and aching for him, and with the newfound sexual confidence he had inspired, she had begun to caress him....

She thought she had pleased him; he had certainly pleasured and satisfied her beyond her wildest dreams. But then she'd had the added impetus of love, which had heightened their union into something far beyond mere sex for her. Thinking back, she realized that Rand hadn't mentioned the word love, not once, not even in the enthralling climax of their passion.

What if it had been just sex to him? Nothing particularly significant, certainly nothing profound, but just a physical urge being satisfied, like an itch being scratched? She felt queasy.

It was painfully paradoxical that since they'd made love she felt less sure of him than she had before. She had taken him inside her, shared intimacies with him she'd known with no one else, but in ceding a part of herself to him, she'd become vulnerable in a way she had never before experienced. The power he wielded over her was frightening to accept. She'd always been so self-assured, so calm and controlled, the mistress of her fate. But now Rand Marshall could determine her happiness or misery.

"I—I hate you, Rand Marshall!" she tried desperately. At that moment, she thought she really did. But she could be persuaded otherwise.

Wordlessly, Rand turned and went inside.

"Oh, smart move, Jamie," Saran said sarcastically. "I know you wanted him to come and grab you so that's why you were yelling nasty things at him, but he thought you meant them. Now what are you going to do?"

"Exactly what I said I was going to do, Saran." Jamie climbed behind the wheel and steered the car carefully from the drive. What choice did she have? her anguished heart cried. He'd made it quite plain that last night had been enough for him; she wasn't worth expending any further effort on. "I'm not going to see him or talk to him again. I intend to—to get on with my life. I'm not the first woman who's ever broken up with a man."

Saran made a sound of disgust and switched on the radio, turning to a rock station and putting the volume so high Jamie felt as if the heavy metal band were playing inside her head. She drove home, greeted the rest of the family, told them in matter-of-fact tones that she'd broken up with Rand, then went upstairs to her room, locked the door and burst into tears.

* * *

Strictly by rote, Rand showered and threw on a pair of black jeans and a black cotton shirt. The clothes fit his mood perfectly, and when the skies turned gray and rain began to fall, it seemed as if even the weather was commiserating with his state of gloom. For the first time in his life, Rand, the cheerful loner by choice who'd always managed to keep his emotions suppressed beyond his level of consciousness, felt the terrible force of loneliness, the desolation of the emptiness that was his life.

He had no one he could really talk to. Jamie had been his first and only true confidant. His friendships were superficial and tinged with competition; he envisioned the astonishment and awkwardness that would transpire if he tried to call one of his friends for consolation. They would uneasily suggest that he call a woman—any woman, hey, they were pretty fungible, weren't they?—and anesthetize his pain with some hot, fast sex. It was the very advice he would have given a few months prior—prior to meeting Jamie and courting her and falling in love with her.

He didn't even think about calling his family. There had never been any encouragement, advice or sympathy from any of them. No, there was no one with whom to share his grief and his confusion. The only person who'd ever cared about him, about how he felt and what he thought and did, was Jamie, and he'd lost her by losing her trust. She thought he had deceived her and she couldn't love him.

He really wasn't surprised that she couldn't. On a gut level, he'd always suspected he was unlovable; his parents and brother, his own flesh and blood, certainly found him so. And he'd been careful never to put his lovability quotient to the test with anyone else. No one but Jamie had ever gotten close enough to really know him—and as the old song went, to know him was to love him, or in his case, to know him was to not love him after all.

When her mother knocked on her bedroom door, Jamie didn't open it. She said, as calmly and politely as possible, that she wasn't feeling well and wanted to stay in her room and try to sleep. She told her father, Grandma, Cassie, Saran, Brandon and Timmy the same thing when each of them knocked. She'd had approximately two hours of solitude and misery when her brother Steve arrived. He'd come home to pick up the shirts that Grandma had laundered and ironed for him—he'd never found a dry cleaner to do his shirts as well as Grandma—and he regularly treated her to the pleasure.

Jamie gave Steve the same controlled little speech she'd given the others, but he was undeterred. Perhaps it was the specter of the locked door that challenged him; no one denied Steve Saraceni anything, even entry to his sister's room. "If you don't open the door this minute, I'm going to break it down," he threatened. "And I'm not kidding."

Jamie knew he wasn't. If she didn't comply, her father would be faced with repairing the door, and Brandon and Timmy would probably attempt to imitate Uncle Steve's door-busting feat every chance they got. Sighing, wiping her tear-filled eyes, Jamie opened the door.

Steve strode into the room, with Cassie and their parents, Grandma and Saran at his heels.

"Saran told us everything, Jamie," her mother said quickly. "And we're so sorry you're upset and we want you to know that we love you."

"Even though we think you're crazy," added Saran. "Breaking up with a hunk like Rand who's cool and smart and rich and—"

"Sweetheart, we respect your right to make your own decisions, of course," Al cut in, "but don't you think you're overreacting a little? I don't see what he did that's so awful."

"Daddy, he lied to me!" cried Jamie, fighting back another surge of tears. Of course it wasn't only that. Although she hadn't told her family so. She'd initially been furious that Rand hadn't told her about his secret life as Brick Lawson, but she didn't consider it an unforgivable sin.

That was a smoke screen; the real issue was that Rand didn't love her. He'd satisfied his curiosity in bed last night and was willing to let her end it between them, choosing any reason she pleased.

"All this fuss because he writes books you don't like?" Grandma seemed incredulous. And quite disapproving. "So you judge and condemn a man because his writing doesn't meet your approval? Sounds like some lunatic ayatollah, not my granddaughter, a librarian in America."

"Grandma, I'm sure there is more to it than that," Cassie interjected quietly. "Jamie loves Rand." She gave her younger sister a sympathetic squeeze. "She has her reasons for doing what she's done. Maybe she had no other choice."

"That's right," Steve chimed in. "I know a prearranged dump when I see one. And that's exactly what's happened here. Marshall is letting Jamie end it between them. Any reason will do, but the bottom line is that he's decided it's over. Here's the scene: there's a fight—it can be over anything, even something as simple as how to boil water—the woman is pushed into saying they're through and the man takes her word for it. Gladly. With incredible relief. Because he *wants* to. Because she was set up to say it. Later, she can change her mind and beg him to take her back but he'll say, 'Sorry, babe. We've reached the point of no return.' "

A ghastly silence descended, then Jamie began to cry again. Having her brother confirm her worst fears dissolved her veneer of self-control. Her heart felt as if it was shattering into a million pieces as pain, the force of which she had never experienced, slashed through her.

Her parents and Cassie crowded around her, hugging her, stroking her, trying to comfort her, near tears themselves. Steve paced back and forth muttering threats, promising vengeance, asking if anyone knew if Rand Marshall had a sister.

"Saran, I need some olive oil to make the rigatoni tonight," said Grandma. "Take me to the store."

"Now?" protested Saran. "Grandma, how can you even think of making dinner when Jamie—"

"So you think we should all starve to death? When six o'clock comes, everybody will want to eat, and we won't if I don't get to the store." The old woman fastened her hand around the girl's arm. "Get Steve's keys, we'll take his car. You drive me right now."

Twelve

Rand stared at the computer screen until his eyes burned. He couldn't write a word. Revising and rewriting was impossible, as well, because he couldn't comprehend what he'd written during previous days. He had decided that writing would be an ideal way to distract himself from the pain, to block it out. Long ago, he'd learned how to put a psychic wall between himself and whatever hurt he was feeling.

He either seemed to have lost that ability or the pain of losing Jamie was too powerful to be banished by a mere act of will. He wandered through the house, sinking deeper and deeper into the terrifying abyss of sorrow and desolation. The telephone rang and he raced to answer it, thinking, hoping, praying that it might be Jamie telling him that it had all been a terrible misunderstanding, that she loved him, that— It wasn't Jamie on the line. It was his mother asking if he'd received the invitation to Dix and Taylor Ann's anniversary party and assuring him that they all understood if he couldn't make it. It was a long drive, he was very busy. Really, the family didn't mind at all if he chose to remain in New Jersey.

Rand gave her the reassurance that she was seeking. No, he wouldn't be coming to Virginia. Yes, it was a long drive and he was very busy with a deadline facing him. His mother ignored the reference to his writing, but the relief in her tone at the promise of his absence was impossible to misinterpret.

Aimless and miserable, he wondered how he was going to get through the next hour. It stretched painfully and endlessly in front of him, and when he thought of all the hours after that, of the interminable nights and days ahead of him, he was deluged by torrents of rage and sorrow, so inextricably mixed that he couldn't begin to separate one from the other. It was as if all the emotions he'd kept pent up for so long had been unleashed, and the force and the strength of them disturbed him.

He tried to fight them, to push his thoughts away, but that old defense didn't work anymore. So he decided to try something else. To blot out his thoughts and exchange his pain for oblivion. He reached for the bottle of Al Saraceni's sour cherry wine, which Jamie's dad had given him on St. Patrick's Day, all those weeks ago.

The first few sips went down like pure fire, with a tinge of tart cherry. Determinedly, he drank some more.

Then the doorbell rang. He had no hopes that it would be Jamie and decided to ignore the bell. Which refused to be ignored. Somebody, one of those demonic little neighborhood salesmen, no doubt, was *leaning* on the bell. Feeling decidedly hostile, clutching the wine bottle in his hand, he threw open the door. "What?" he roared, determined to scare the intrusive little harasser away forever.

He got the shock of his life. For standing on his doorstep, her thumb firmly on the doorbell, was Jamie's grandmother with Saran close behind her. Rand was aghast. Not only had he snarled at her—Jamie's grandmother!—he was unshaven, his hair was uncombed and he was clutching the wine bottle like a drunken sailor.

"Just answer me one question," Grandma said, her dark eyes snapping and fierce. "Was it a prearranged dump?"

Jamie knew that Cassie and her parents were trying to cheer her up, but a trip to the multiscreen cinema at the mall with Timmy and Brandon to see the latest Disney cartoon release was not going to work. And the thought of watching cartoon characters cavort across the screen was fairly mind-boggling. So she declined, but urged them to go ahead without her, and was surprised when Grandma and Saran decided to go along, too. She couldn't remember Grandma ever going to a movie, although she'd once heard her grandmother mention seeing *Gone With the Wind*...during its first release in 1939.

But Jamie didn't question them; she even suspected that they were all eager for an excuse to escape from the house after having to endure her moping and weeping all day. She didn't really want to be alone, though, and almost asked Steve if he would stay and keep her company. She decided against it when he received phone calls from the three young women with whom he'd made dates for that night. He planned to split the evening among them, staging strategic quarrels to end each date early. Whoever he decided to favor with his presence for the entire night would then be the lucky recipient of his makeup call.

After hearing that, Jamie was too incensed on the women's behalf to want her brother in the same town with her, let alone the same house. So she sat alone in the family room, if one can be alone with seven cats sharing the same sofa, and tried to read. For the first time, she had trouble selecting a book. Romances made her cry, mysteries involved too much concentration from her aching mind, so she settled for one of Grandma's true crime books, about a bloodthirsty clan who kept trying to kill each other off for insurance money.

The sound of the doorbell was a welcome relief. She put down her book and hurried to answer the door. Rand was standing on the other side of it.

His hand snaked out to encircle her wrist. "You're coming with me," he said in a bold tone that brooked no argument.

Jamie brooked it anyway. "I am not! You can't come here and—"

"I was invited here."

"Not by me!" Her heart was pounding, her stomach had begun to somersault, and her voice was embarrassingly squeaky. Breathless at the sight of him, she was unable to summon the irate fury his arrogant assertion demanded.

"By your grandmother and Saran. They came to visit me this afternoon."

"Oh, no!" Jamie groaned. "They had no right to interfere."

"Grandma said a family has every right to interfere when one member is making another one miserable." He smiled wryly. "She said she considered me family. And the feeling is mutual. For the first time in my life I feel like I know what it's like to belong to a family."

Jamie scowled at him. "All the interference and inconvenience—"

"Yeah, there's that. But there's involvement and support and fun, too." He gave her wrist a tug. "Let's go, Jamie. We have a lot to talk about."

Her eyes filled with sudden tears, which she tried to blink away. "I don't know what my grandmother said to you."

"She said you were crying your eyes out in your room because you loved me and thought that I didn't love you," he said bluntly.

Jamie winced. What was the use in denying it? But her fighting spirit, though severely dashed, was still viable. "So you came over to offer your condolences?" She managed a very credible glare. "Or to gloat?"

Rand grinned. "I knew I could count on you not to give in without a struggle." Swiftly, smoothly, he scooped her up in his arms, turning slightly to pull the front door closed behind them.

"Oh!" Jamie gasped. Reflexively, her arms encircled his neck. She felt disoriented by her unexpected loss of equilibrium. It was strange, being carried, she thought dazedly. The dependence, the complete loss of control... "Put me down!" she demanded, though her voice was not as forceful as she had intended.

"Your wish is my command." He slowly lowered her to her feet beside the passenger door of the Ferrari, letting her slide against the length of his body, turning the release into a sensuous caress. Before she could move away from him, he locked his arms around her and held her tight. "But I'm taking you home with me tonight, baby. We're going to make up and make love and—"

"I won't go to bed with you!"

"You already have. And you loved every minute of it." He touched his lips to the sensitive curve of her neck, then nipped lightly with his teeth. His big hand moved up and down her back before sliding slowly to her bottom, where he sensuously kneaded the rounded softness. "And so did I, my love. Ah, Jamie, you evoke feelings in me that I never dreamed I possessed, that I didn't think I was capable of experiencing. I tried to tell you so last night. I thought I had, but—" he lifted his lips and stared into her deep blue eyes "—obviously, I failed to let you know how much you mean to me, how much I care."

Jamie closed her eyes as a rush of emotion so intense it was dizzying poured through her. She clung to him, her knees weak, her head spinning. "You let me walk away," she whispered. "You didn't try to make me stay. When Saran told you not to let me go, you s-said that forcible seduction wasn't your style."

He brushed her mouth with his. "And there you were, hoping to be forcibly seduced?"

Her face turned crimson. "I'm not in the mood to be teased!" She began to struggle indignantly. "Let me go, Rand."

"No way. I learn from my mistakes, honey. You just told me that if I hadn't let you go earlier today we could've avoided a day in hell. And so—"

He clamped his mouth over hers, and when she opened her mouth to protest, his tongue darted between her parted lips, filling her mouth and claiming it in a fiercely demanding, possessive kiss. Jamie's arms crept around his neck, and her body arched instinctively, fitting her soft feminine curves against the hard planes of his masculine frame as she responded to him with all the vibrance and passion of her nature.

"I love you, Jamie," he said huskily, as they held each other, panting and breathless with emotion and arousal. "There's never been anyone like you in my life. I took one look at you in the library that day and lost my head. Not long afterward I lost my heart to you, too. Everything I've done and said since then has been to keep you with me. Forever, Jamie."

"You love me," she repeated softly and felt the tears begin to slide down her cheeks. She'd never cried so much in her entire life as she had today, but these tears were different, they were tears of joy and relief and sheer emotional release. "Oh, Rand, I love you, too. I've loved you for such a long time and I thought—I hoped—that you were falling in love with me, too. And last night was—"

"Perfect," Rand cut in, holding her tightly against him. "I felt a happiness, a sense of completeness I'd never known. So when Daniel showed up at the door, blathering about that damn bet—"

"I know there wasn't a bet, Rand." It was her turn to interrupt. "Not on your end, anyway. As for your writing as Brick Lawson, I'm sorry I made it impossible for you to tell me. Now that I know it's you who has written those books, I know I'm going to love them."

Rand laughed. "Honey, you don't have to go that far. You don't even have to read them. I just want you to love me, Jamie. And to marry me. Your grandmother called the Sons of Italy hall from my place this afternoon and booked our wedding reception for the beginning of August. Will you do it, Jamie? Will you marry me?"

"Oh, Rand, yes!" she cried exultantly. He lifted her off her feet and exuberantly swung her around in circles as she laughed and cried with happiness.

The drive from her house to his was a joyous one, as they made plans for their wedding, for their future, teasing and laughing and kissing hotly at each and every stop sign and red light. Rand carried Jamie into the house and directly to his bedroom. She clung to him, trembling with anticipation and arousal.

"I love you, Rand," she said as he gently lowered her to the bed. It was both a pledge and a promise.

"And I love you, my darling." Rand began to undress her, taking the time to kiss and caress her after he removed each garment. By the time she was naked, hot ribbons of pleasure were streaking through her. Rand quickly pulled off his own clothes, and she assisted him with eager hands.

He drew her into his arms for a long, lusty kiss, while they sensually explored each other, reexperiencing the pleasures of last night while making new and exciting erotic discoveries about each other.

He positioned her to receive him, his eyes holding hers, and a slow, sexy smile curved his lips as he merged their bodies with a sure, masterful stroke.

Jamie cried his name again and again as he moved within her, savoring the full feeling of him inside her, loving the emotional and physical intimacy they were sharing. His deep, slow strokes accelerated into a hard, fast rhythm that made her move for him and with him as the pleasurable, powerful tension built and grew, finally exploding into paroxysms of white-hot rapture. The force of her climax triggered his own, and Rand was thrust over the edge into ecstasy, losing himself in her and the binding passion of their love.

They lay in each other's arms, replete and wonderfully sated as they slowly, languidly drifted to earth from the rapturous heights of passion. "I'm so glad we made up, Rand," Jamie murmured, gazing at him with warm, limpid eyes. "I don't think I could've managed to get through the night, thinking that you didn't love me." A small shudder quivered through her at the terrible prospect.

"I thought you couldn't love me, that it wasn't possible for me to keep your love," he confessed haltingly. "And then I read chapter six in that damn courtship book and it was all about fighting and breaking up and knowing when to let go and face the fact that it's over. I felt as if it had been written especially for me."

"Oh, Rand, we're going to fight from time to time, all couples do, but let's make a vow never to walk away from each other again," Jamie whispered passionately, intensely, hugging him tight. "So that no matter how mad we might get at each other, we'll know deep down that our fight will end in us making up and not breaking up."

"Jamie, that's a promise I'm happy to make."

The sincerity in his voice and the love in his eyes brought emotional tears to her eyes. "I love you so much, Rand. I'll never leave you, ever. I promise." It was a pledge as binding and as irrefutable as the wedding vows she would take in August.

Rand knew it and made one of his own. "And I'll never let you go. We're together forever, Jamie." He smiled, feeling almost light-headed with happiness. And jubilant enough to tease her. "So you're going to stick with me, even after you read the reviews of my next book?"

"I certainly am. And I'm going to read all your books and love them," she insisted with her characteristic determination. "From now on, I'm a rabid Brick Lawson fan."

"Fair enough," Rand said, caressing her arousingly, lovingly as passion flamed between them once more. "Because I've always been an ardent, devoted, impassioned, adoring Jamie Saraceni fan.''

"Your mind really is a virtual thesaurus," Jamie marveled, and then her mouth claimed his for an ardent, devoted, impassioned, adoring kiss.

* * * * *

SILHOUETTE® *Desire*

COMING NEXT MONTH

#559 SUNSHINE—Jo Ann Algermissen
A Florida alligator farm? It was just what ad exec Rob Emery *didn't* need! But sharing the place with Angelica Franklin made life with the large lizards oh, so appealing....

#560 GUILTY SECRETS—Laura Leone
Leah McCargar sensed sexy houseguest Adam Jordan was not *all* he claimed. But before she could prove him guilty of lying, she became guilty...of love.

#561 THE HIDDEN PEARL—Celeste Hamilton
Aunt Eugenia's final match may be her toughest! Can Jonah Pendleton coax shy Maggie O'Grady into leading a life of adventure? The next book in the series *Aunt Eugenia's Treasures*.

#562 LADIES' MAN—Raye Morgan
Sensible Trish Becker knew that Mason Ames was nothing more than a good-looking womanizer! But she still couldn't stop herself from succumbing to his seductive charms.

#563 KING OF THE MOUNTAIN—Joyce Thies
Years ago Gloria Hubbard had learned that rough, tough William McCann was one untamable man. Now he was back in town...and back in her life.

#564 SCANDAL'S CHILD—Ann Major
When May's *Man of the Month* Officer Garret Cagan once again saved scandalous Noelle Martin from trouble, the Louisiana bayou wasn't the only thing steaming them up....

AVAILABLE NOW:

#553 HEAT WAVE
Jennifer Greene

#554 PRIVATE PRACTICE
Leslie Davis Guccione

#555 MATCHMAKER, MATCHMAKER
Donna Carlisle

#556 MONTANA MAN
Jessica Barkley

#557 THE PASSIONATE ACCOUNTANT
Sally Goldenbaum

#558 RULE BREAKER
Barbara Boswell

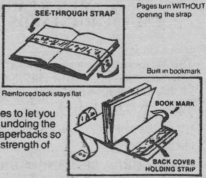